TRAIL OF THE REAPER

Bounty-hunter Jonathan Grimm — the man they called the Reaper — took a break from his man-hunting to attend a family wedding. But a shooting on the doorstep hurled him back into his man-chasing role. Then, what started out as a straightforward chase ran him smack into hard-case gunmen aiming to cut him down. At the tail end of his life, how could he afford to keep tangling with younger, trigger-happy gunnies? But one thing was a dead cert — before the last man was left standing, a lot of lead was going to fly.

B. J. HOLMES

TRAIL OF THE REAPER

Complete and Unabridged

LINFORD
Leicester

First published in Great Britain in 2004 by
Robert Hale Limited
London

First Linford Edition
published 2005
by arrangement with
Robert Hale Limited
London

British Library CIP Data

Holmes, B. J.
    Trail of the reaper.—Large print ed.—
Linford western library
    1. Western stories
    2. Large type books
    I. Title
    823.9'14 [F]

    ISBN 1–84395–877–5

Published by
F. A. Thorpe (Publishing)
Anstey, Leicestershire

Set by Words & Graphics Ltd.
Anstey, Leicestershire
Printed and bound in Great Britain by
T. J. International Ltd., Padstow, Cornwall

This book is printed on acid-free paper

For Helen C.

1

The batwings flew open and a tall figure clumped through, shaking the rain from his slicker. He took off his Stetson and flicked away the excess moisture, then settled the hat back on his head.

'Delivery. Got three barrels of beer on the wagon.'

The bartender looked up from his task of swamping the counter and eyed the newcomer.

'Ledgers' Brewery?'

'The very same.'

'What's happened to Charlie, the usual driver?'

'Down with a chill. Reckon this goddamn wet weather's finally got through to him.'

The bartender nodded. 'Poor Charlie.' Then, his already wry expression became even more quizzical, as he added, 'Hang on, we ain't expecting no delivery till next week.'

'Don't know nothing about that, pal. I'm just a driver doing as he's told. Check it out with your boss.'

As the bartender left, the newcomer looked across at the saloon's lone customer, seated at the far end.

'Say, mister,' the rain-sodden man said. 'I'd deem it right helpful if you could maybe give me a hand with the unloading. I've had one hell of a day. Three barrels is all.'

The man took a swig from his glass and looked dismissively at the tall figure, whose slicker was still puddling the boards.

'Tell you what, old-timer — I'll give you some help in *drinking* it,' he sniggered. 'Whatever you've brung couldn't be worse than this sour mash. But as to exerting myself heaving kegs, no deal.' He raised his hands and inspected them. 'Can't risk damaging these delicate mitts of mine.'

The other shrugged and casually

walked along the bar, his head angling as he looked the premises over: the smoke-stained ceiling, the rough-hewn timber walls.

But when the visitor disappeared behind him, the seated man suddenly felt uneasy. There was something wrong here. But what the hell was it? For some seconds he couldn't figure it out. *Clump, clump* to his rear, the boots trod the boards. Yeah, there was something odd. Then it hit him: this guy was supposed to be a wagon-driver — yet as he walked, *spurs* jingled. No wagon-driver needed spurs!

On the realization, he whirled round — only to find himself facing the business end of a long-barrelled .44. Behind the gun was a face, a face that told a tale. The lines in the jowls, and the long greying hair, hinted that their owner would never see sixty again. And the scattering of black powder-burns high on his cheekbone, near his eyes, suggested he was more familiar with gundowns than wagon-driving. The piercing eyes told the story of a man who lived by seeing. They told of determination, of ruthlessness; traits all of which were emphasized by the arthritic but experienced thumb clicking back the hammer.

The seated man's face blanched. It was the powder-burnt cheekbone that clinched it.

'It can't be. The Reaper. You're . . . dead.'[1]

The other ignored the comment.

'We can do this the easy way or the hard way. The easy way, you let me take your gun. I'm gonna do it real slow, and you don't — '

But before the completion of the sentence, the seated man made a grab at the barrel. The gunman drove his fist forward, simultaneously raising the barrel so that the sharp underside edge of the butt rammed into the man's forehead, whacking him

---

[1] For why he should think this, see *A Coffin for the Reaper*.

backwards from the chair.

The blow, if delivered in earlier years, would have been enough to put out its recipient. However, while the action did serve to knock the man back, now put into effect by ageing sinews it did not render him unconscious.

The man crashed to the floor and in a flowing movement rolled beneath the table, hauling on his own gun. He fired — but from below the table all he could see now were the old man's legs, and the slug sliced harmlessly through the bottom of the fellow's slicker.

He up-ended the table for cover, and continued throwing lead.

But the old man had dived sideways to the floor, giving him enough sighting around the tipped table. With an arm stretched along the boards, he triggered twice. Travelling at fifteen hundred feet a second — and at close range — the bullets made a hell of a mess. Bloodied hair chunked away as the first slug channelled along the side of the man's skull. The second blasted a red hole in his chest.

The newcomer got to his feet and rolled the table aside so he could get a good look at the inert figure.

'OK, your choice,' he sighed. 'The hard way.'

There was a noise to the side, and he whirled round, his gun ready.

It was the saloon-owner coming from the back, croaking 'Jesus Christ!' at the sight that met his eyes.

The visitor saw no threat, so sheathed his gun and eased himself slowly into a chair. His knee was sore from hitting the hard boards, and his leg muscles ached from the stresses put on them. Worse, his knuckles pained. He looked at his right hand. Lately, the joints, especially at the base of his trigger finger, had been swelling badly and giving him some gyp. As he rubbed the offending node, the bartender and the saloon-owner came from behind the bar, advanced hesitantly.

'Hey, what the hell's going on,

mister?' the white-faced saloon-owner queried.

The gunman pulled back his slicker. He rummaged around and withdrew a document, which he handed across.

'You got a wanted man on the premises. Rafe Petrie. And this is he, or what's left of him. I'm taking him in.'

The saloon-man surveyed the mangled corpse. 'Did you have to do that to him?'

'We had a point of difference on the matter of me taking him in.'

The other perused the Wanted poster and handed it back. 'You law?'

'Kind of.'

'Bounty-hunter?'

'If you like.'

'So you ain't got no beer out there?' the bartender put in.

'No, but I'd sure like one.'

Minutes later, Jonathan Grimm was seated with a glass, his gaze still on the crumpled figure. Why did they always push their luck?

He put his head back and rubbed

his knuckles again. With long-awaited refreshment at his elbow, and his behind saddle-weary, he was in no hurry.

That is, no *immediate* hurry; but he did have places to go. When he had assuaged his initial thirst, he went outside and returned with a tarped bundle. At the door he shook off the damp and returned to his chair. He undid the wrapping to reveal a chart, which he laid out on the table.

He put on his glasses and took out his smoking-pouch. He stuffed his briar and lit up while he studied the map. In any other circumstances he would have taken Petrie to the Federal Office in Territorial Capital. He ran his finger over the map. Normally there would be no problem, but he had a commitment to be in Lobo Wells within the week, and the big city would be too much of a detour. Not only was he short on time, but also he needed the money; and bounty payments could only be made by Federal authorities.

'Where's the nearest Federal Marshal?' he asked, looking back over his glasses to the bar.

The saloon-man thought for a moment, then said, 'That'd be Jersey Creek.'

Grimm peered through the lenses again and nodded with satisfaction when he'd picked out the name on the chart. It was a few hours' ride along the route to Lobo Wells.

* * *

The Jersey Creek lawman looked at the tall, gaunt oldster in front of him. The man had announced himself as Jonathan Grimm. Of course, from the time he had been a kid the marshal had heard of the legendary bounty-chaser — who hadn't? — but had assumed he was long dead. Might just as well be, by his appearance — looming, skeletal — like death on legs.

The spectre unravelled a poster on the counter to reveal the surly, pig-like features of his captive.

'Rafe Petrie,' he explained. 'One and a half grand. He's outside.'

The lawman nodded in receipt of the information. 'Bring him in.'

'You'll thank me if I don't. Figure you'll not want him smelling out the premises. Besides, he ain't capable of making it to the boardwalk.'

The marshal picked up the dodger and followed the bounty-hunter outside. Grimm pulled up the head by its hair so that the lawman could compare the features with the poster.

'Yup, ain't gainsaying they's one and the same, Mr Grimm. There's a little difference between 'em, of course. The one on the poster has got his eyes open and ain't got a gash in his forehead. But don't suppose you can have everything.'

'Let's say we had ourselves an altercation with regard to the issue of his accompanying me to your establishment.'

The lawman raised an eyebrow at the hunter's choice of words, then said,

'OK. I formally confirm it's Petrie.' He gestured to one of the bystanders in the growing crowd, telling him to fetch the mortician.

Minutes later, Petrie was on his way to a box in the funeral parlour and the two men were back in the law office having a java around the stove.

'I'm in a hurry, Marshal,' Grimm said. 'How long to conclude our business?'

'Well, I have to get clearance from Territorial Capital.'

'I know the ropes, but that's a formality.'

'A formality mebbe, but a formality that has to be complied with.'

The man known as the Reaper sighed resignedly. 'OK, how long will it take?'

The lawman looked at the calendar on the wall.

'It's late, Friday afternoon. Those city-types live in a different world. Most places out there will have closed up store by this time. Figure the earliest will be Monday. That's if they move their asses. You know what pen-pushers are like. Especially government pen-pushers. But, I guess, you should have the cash in your hand by midweek.'

'Midweek? Jeez, I got business elsewhere.'

The lawman pondered. 'Well, if you gotta be travelling, I could put the bounty on hold in the bank here in town until I get clearance. Then you could collect it as soon as you can get back.'

'I'm not only in a hurry,' Grimm said, 'but I need the money too. Like now.'

The man said nothing. Grimm had no recourse but to give the matter thought. Then he said, 'Got an idea that will do us both some good. OK, you know how the system works; and you know that regional headquarters will sanction payment. So, my suggestion is you rustle up some cash here and now. Then, you give me a receipt that you've received the merchandise — namely, our mutual acquaintance Petrie over the road — and pay me twelve hundred. I sign that I've received the full amount of fifteen hundred. Then, when the money comes through you keep it all, making yourself three hundred bucks.'

The lawman thought. 'Twelve hundred? Can't raise that amount at such short notice.' He thought some more, and a look came to his eye; the glint that can be discerned in a coyote's eye when he sees a cottontail out in the open. 'I'll do it for half,' he concluded.

Grimm wearily shook his head. 'Too big a cut, pilgrim. And I need a round figure. In my book, that's at least a thousand dollars.'

'Why a round figure?'

'That ain't the issue here.'

The lawman sniffed noisily. Then: 'OK, I'll see if I can pull it together.'

'You do that. I'll be in the saloon.'

Grimm moseyed over to the drinking-parlour, took a beer and sat near the batwings. He stuffed his briar with tobacco, lit up, and contemplated his situation. He'd already lost the big dollars in this caper.[1] Worse, there was nothing in the pipeline, so he'd figured one and a half smackeroos was better than a kick in the keester. On the plus side, it hadn't been difficult to trail and nab Petrie. With news out that Grimm was dead, Petrie had not been concerned about covering his backtrail or working up a lather on his horse. The hunter ruminated on the sheriff's proposal. OK, he was going to lose five hundred on the deal . . . what the hell.

One drink and one pipe on, the lawman made an appearance at the door of the saloon. The two men walked back to the office, where the officer counted out five hundred dollars on his desk.

'That's all I can pull together, pal.'

'Five hundred?'

The sheriff said nothing.

Grimm was no fool, and knew the bozo was grifting him. He'd got the

---

[1] See *A Coffin for the Reaper*.

measure of the fellow as soon as he'd met him, and the further short-changing came as no surprise. But he hadn't expected it to be quite such a whack. He thought on the alternatives, then said: 'OK, if that's it, that's it. Let's exchange documents, so I can get moving.'

Once more on the back of his beloved Andalusian, he hit the trail. He had a long way to go — to Lobo Wells and a wedding. As 'father' of the bride, he had wanted his gift to be the best, and his bounty of fifteen hundred on Petrie was to have been his wedding present. Instead, he had ended up with a mere five hundred in his wallet.

Mere? Hell, he mused, the happy couple could raise a mortgage with such a sum! Maybe even buy a small house, picket fence and all.

And with that thought, he didn't feel so bad.

2

He reined in and took out his chart, then surveyed the spare, dry land. To save time he had cut across country, following no trails. It was several days on and, although the territory was new to him, he knew from his map that he was getting close to Lobo Wells. Less than a day's ride; plenty of time to make his appointment two days hence.

Trouble was, it was late in the day and the sky had been darkening with ugly thunderheads. He rolled up his chart and pressed on.

But the ominous clouds dogged him with the same kind of vengeful tenacity with which he'd so recently pursued the outlaw Petrie.

When they came, the first raindrops were not bad, mere irritating spits. The terrain was wild and lonely, with no obvious places for shelter, so when the spits became hard splatters he drew rein and pulled on his slicker. It was dry country, a land where rain didn't come often — but when it came, boy, it came. Nothing for it but to press on, with head bent low, hat-brim sagging, and the rain drumming on his shoulders.

The horse's state was miserable as it was, so he let it take its head. Only now and again did the man glance up to take stock. Then, through the blurring sheets of rain, he could make out the square shape of a shack.

When he got close he reined in, wiped his eyes and looked through the watery veil. The place was dilapidated, but looked as though it would provide adequate shelter. More important, against its side he could identify the vestiges of an awning.

He dismounted, and made a circuit of the building. Most of the windows still retained glass. He moved around, peering through each in turn. No sign of life. He took out his gun and kicked open the door. Cautiously, he edged through the entrance.

Then he returned to his cherished Andalusian. In its autumn years, it still had a striking appearance.

'Vacant possession, pardner,' he told the animal. 'The place is ours.'

He gave the awning the once-over. Rain was spattering through some cracks, but there was a section in the middle that was dry, with enough good space for the horse. He tied the animal to a rail. He took off the saddle and accoutrements, and heaved them inside the building.

He took out a rag and returned to his mount to give him a good rub-down. Finally, he tipped some of the oats that he carried for emergencies into a nosebag.

With the horse settled in a modicum of comfort, he returned inside.

There was enough detritus lying about to provide kindling, and he started a fire going in the stove. When it had got a grip, he dashed out into the rain, pulled some slats from a crumbling fence and, back inside, stacked them against a wall to drain for later use.

With no lamps, the interior was dark, but in time the fire of the stove gave enough illumination for him to set about his tasks. He returned to his horse, gave him a last rub-down and threw a dry blanket across his back.

Back indoors, he hung his slicker on a hook, then shucked off his wet overclothes, draping them on the back of a chair near the stove.

'All the comforts of home,' he mused, as he settled to a meal of jerky and hardtack in front of the glowing stove.

Finally, with his slicker dripping pools on the wooden boards, he laid blankets on the floor near the stove. He angled a slat of wood against the door, to act as a warning of anyone entering. Ensuring his gun was handy, he bedded down to listen to the rain drumming on the roof. And in no time he became a snoring heap.

★   ★   ★

The merest creaking of the planking outside was enough to rouse him. In a split second he was leaning on his elbow, gun levelled — even before the warning slat against the door crashed to the floor. The door swung open, and he saw a short figure outlined against the glistening night rain.

'Whoever's at home, don't worry,' a voice croaked. 'It's only Ol' Barnaby.' The man clattered in, closed the door and shook off surplus water. 'Saw the hoss, so I knew somebody was in occupancy.'

Even though it was dark, the fellow obviously knew the geography because he easily found a seat by the table. Grimm's hand tightened on his .44 as he heard the fellow rooting through a warbag. But it was a small oil-lamp rather than a weapon that the visitor brought forth, which he then proceeded to light. Eventually its glow revealed a wizened old man, who regarded the other in silence.

'Just passing through,' Grimm explained.

'Didn't think the place belonged to anyone.'

'It don't. Been derelict for years. Mainly only me that uses it, and that's only now and again. Occasionally, passing folks like you will avail themselves of its facilities.' He chuckled. 'But it's real luxury for a fiddle-footed bum like me. Everything an itinerant wants. Huh, even got its own privy out back!'

Grimm stood up, still keeping his gun ready and claimed some wood to re-stoke the fire.

'Ain't often a traveller finds derelict places in such a reasonable condition,' he said.

The old man nodded. 'It's being way off any trails, you see. Few folks have reason to come this way.' He laughed. 'Figure I could leave ten dollars on the table and it would be there six months later. That's if ever I had ten dollars!'

'I've had some coffee on the go. I'll heat it up.'

'That'll be most welcome, friend. Real miserable night out there. Damn rain plays jimmy-hell with my rheuma-tism.'

'Tell me about it,' Grimm replied, aware of his own aching joints.

For a while, the newcomer busied himself with making his own prepara-tions to turn in.

'Used to be a mine just up the hill apiece,' he said when he'd got a cup of steaming coffee before him. 'The Red Mountain Mine. But like many such ventures, didn't last long. Soon got played out. Same story all over the West — from boom to bust in six months.'

Gun hidden but ready, Grimm settled back under his blanket. He still had some travelling to do, and needed his shut-eye.

'There was a couple of buildings,' the old man went on. 'The other one was up near the mine entrance. That disappeared under a landslide. This un's the only one left standing.'

Grimm's eyes were drooping. If the old codger could bottle his droning, he could make a fortune marketing it as a snake-oil sleeping-draught.

'Mind, Red Mountain ain't even a mountain, just a hill is all. Wonder why we Westerners have to exaggerate everything? We see a gopher mound and we call it a mountain. Same with cities. Back in the old country, place has got to have a cathedral reaching into the clouds before folks are allowed to designate their place a city. Here, two false-fronts are thrown up in a day on either side of the trail and you got a 'city'.'

Grimm shook his head to try to keep awake. He would not feel easy until the other man was asleep — but when would that be?

'Yeah,' the fellow droned on, 'this place was built at a time when Indians were still uppity.'

He got up and tottered behind the stove. He pulled some matting out of the way and tapped the floor. 'Most folks don't know about this.'

He fiddled and wheezed, and eventually raised a trapdoor. 'You know what this is, pilgrim? Escape route for when redskins were whooping and a-hollering outside.' He looked into the depths for a moment. 'Tunnel goes right down to the arroyo out back. Reckon this has some stories to tell.'

He clattered the thing back in place, and pulled the matting over it.

And that was about the last thing Grimm remembered before he lost his battle with sleep.

* * *

He awoke in a room filled with body smells, dawn light creeping across the cobwebbed ceiling. He glanced across to see the oldster snoring deeply on the far side. The rain had exhausted itself, and the fire was burnt out. He grunted into arousal and rose in preparation for the resumption of his journey.

He stretched, and had just checked the set of his gunbelt when a voice behind him said, 'Them's sure fancy irons.'

24

He turned to see a bleary-eyed old man, leaning on his elbow, looking at him.

'Morning, Barnaby,' he rejoined.

'Them shooters — they just for appearances,' the fellow went on, 'or can you use 'em?'

Grimm patted his pistols. 'I can use 'em. why?'

'Point is, you aiming to lit out *without* grub in your belly?'

'Got some jerky and hardtack. You're welcome to a bite.'

'Hell, that ain't enough vitals for a growing younker like yourself.'

Younker? Grimm thought. There probably weren't three months between the two of them!

'This time of morning, down in the arroyo,' the other continued, 'it's teeming with cottontails and jack-rabbits. Breakfast automatically laid on. If God had not chose to empty his heavens on us last night, I'd have set some wire nooses down there afore I hit the sack, as is my usual habit. As it was,

I'd plumb reconciled myself to the fact that that was not to be.'

He scratched at his body and yawned. 'On the other hand, if you know how to look down a gun-sight and can pull a good trigger, we should be able to start the day with meat in our guts. What d'you say, youngster?'

Sounded too good to resist. Grimm leant down and pulled his rifle from its scabbard. 'Lead the way, mister.'

The sky was lighting up as they moved outside. Grimm said howdy to his horse, checked he was OK, then followed the old man down the slope.

Approaching the arroyo, they bellied down and inched towards the edge. There were touches of green in the dried-out watercourse, most of the dampness from the previous day already having been absorbed.

The oldster was right. It was a veritable menagerie: apart from rabbits, there were prairie chickens, even a skunk and a raccoon, each creature intent on finding its own breakfast.

'Spoilt for choice,' Grimm breathed.

Two fast shots and the arroyo was empty, save for two dead cottontails. He eased himself down into the hollow, and picked up the small carcasses by their ears.

'Ain't a deal of meat on 'em,' he said, having given them the once-over, 'but leastways there's one each.'

The other joined him, and relieved him of his small burdens. He held them up and made his own assessment of their culinary potential. He was just about to move away when he pointed with his free hand. 'There, that tunnel I was telling you about last night.'

Grimm vaguely remembered the man's ramblings and the noisy trapdoor from the previous night, when all he had sought was sleep. He looked in the indicated direction, but couldn't see anything obvious.

The old man moved across to a clump of brush at the side, and pulled at the vegetation. Grimm wasn't really interested but joined him and made a pretence of investigating the hole that had been revealed.

'Leads right back to the trapdoor at the shack,' the other said. 'Like I showed you last night. Must have saved a few lives in its day.'

'Guess so,' Grimm added, out of politeness, and headed for the arroyo wall, eager to get going. He had some miles to get behind him.

Back at the shack, the oldster laid the rabbits on the planking of the veranda and went inside.

'Start a fire. I see you collected enough wood last night for a good blaze. And we need some bale wire. You should find some about the place.'

Grimm saluted with an exaggerated 'Yes, sir' and a smile. He hadn't been given orders since his army days.

The other took a knife from his warbag and returned outside. He made a slit at the back of the first rabbit, and tore off its skin with one practised movement. Within seconds he had dis-embowelled both creatures and slung the innards away.

'Yes, sirree — ain't nothing like the smell of cooked cottontail first thing in the morning.'

Later, with a full belly and a fully fledged sun on the rise, Jonathan Grimm headed out at a canter.

3

The journey continued without inci-
dent. In the old days, he would have
made many miles without a break. But,
like him, his long-serving Andalusian
had seen fitter times, so rest-ups
became more frequent.

On one such occasion he took out his
chart. A while back he'd cut a well-used
trail, and now had come to a crossing.
As it was the only intersection in the
vicinity on the map, he could locate his
position with some certainty. Not much
further to Gulch City, the last town
before his destination of Lobo Wells.

Back in the saddle, he ruminated on
the prospect of seeing Sarah again. It
had been some ten years since he'd
seen her, and their acquaintance had
not begun in the most propitious
circumstances. Sarah Toomey she'd
been then. He hadn't known of her

existence when he had been trailing her father, up in the timber country of the Ouachita Mountains.

Hanging Judge Parker had initiated a new campaign to wipe out the legion of owlhoots who infested the Indian-held lands of Arkansas. Although the US marshal's force had a complement of two hundred officers, the judge had been so eager to see the operation through quickly that he had made it known he welcomed the help of bounty-hunters. Presenting himself at Fort Smith, Grimm had been informed by the high sheriff that there was a pork barrel of dollars for anybody who fetched in Red Toomey, who was known to be holed up in the mountains.

He had been on Toomey's trail for a week when he finally tracked him down to the shack that served as his hideout. But the outlaw threw a hail of lead, to make it plain he wasn't being taken. The man known as the Reaper finished the stand-off with one heart shot. But that wasn't the end of his troubles.

His mind went back . . .

He heard the shack door creak to his side, and he whirled round, one of his army .44s ready to mete out bloody deserts to yet another hardcase. Just in time, he stopped himself putting pressure on the hair-trigger.

In the doorway stood a young girl. She wore a brown cloth pelisse, cut plain and straight, hooked and eyed down the front, fastened at the waist with a cord. It was difficult to tell her age with any exactitude. The pelisse masked her figure, and the features of her face were barely discernible, deep in the shadow of a drab bonnet. But she was small, less than four feet; that alone indicated tender years.

'Pa!' she screamed, and run past Grimm, dropping on to the fallen man — the man whom the bounty-hunter had just despatched to hell and beyond with one clean shot through the heart.

'Judas Priest,' Grimm mouthed to himself. He couldn't remember the

tally of no-goods he'd killed during his career, but this — shooting a man in front of his own kid — this was a new marble to pull out of the bag. He breathed deeply, tensely, as the bottom dropped out of his stomach. Sickened, he watched the girl pull at the lifeless limbs, trying to hold up the slack head of her father. When she saw the blood, she made an animal noise and recoiled.

'You killed him! You killed Pa!' She turned, faced Grimm directly so that he could more easily make out the infant features. And the accusing eyes. 'Why?'

It had not been the time for lengthy explanations. There was a commonplace expression, overused to the point of being meaningless, but it was short, so he gave it.

'It was him or me, missy.'

Voiced like that, it sounded weak, like some whining pretext, but it was true. Red Toomey had been around some — and knew full well the no-nonsense attitude of the bounty-hunter known as the Reaper. The chips

33

down, his only choice was facing a rope or being gunned down by Grimm, unless he could somehow blast his way out of it. Which he had tried to do.

True or not, it didn't matter. The little girl didn't hear. She just said, 'Why? Why?' In her eyes, for a moment, Grimm could see the total sum of the hate of all the kin and friends of every man he'd ever killed . . .

So he had been stuck with a kid — a kid whose father he had gunned down; stuck in the middle of nowhere, half-way up a mountain. The two of them were to go through many adventures together[1] before the hate in the little girl's eyes had dissipated — when she came to realize something about the rights and wrongs of the world. Indeed, in time, her eyes began to reflect a modicum of affection for the leathery, old curmudgeon who had become her benefactor.

---

[1] These escapades are recounted in *Blood on the Reaper*.

Learning that her mother had no interest in taking her on, Grimm had looked elsewhere. Eventually he had managed to place her with a couple, Jim and Hester Stanhope, who had recently lost their son, not much older than Sarah. And that was the last he'd seen of her, standing on the Stanhopes' porch clutching a ragdoll — as he'd ridden off in search of yet another law-breaking renegade.

Years later, at one of his post boxes, he'd come across a letter from her. Having no permanent home himself, he was a difficult man to locate, and the letter was six months old. It just asked how he was and passed on family news. She must have been around thirteen then. From that time on, they'd undertaken infrequent but regular correspondence. So at least she knew her old protector was alive. And through this method he learned of her schooling and growing-up, and of daily life on the Stanhope homestead. It was in this way that, a year ago, he'd learned of Jim

Stanhope's passing.

Then, out of the blue, a letter had turned up, telling of Sarah's impending wedding. A whole page was taken up in description of how wonderful was Frank, her intended. Not only that, Grimm being the only remaining elderly male in her 'family', he had been invited to fulfil the function of giving her away.

Not being a social creature, Grimm had been daunted by the prospect, but realized that Sarah was the only 'family' he had, too, and so he had replied that he would be honoured.

As he rode, he pondered on how she might look now, and wondered whether he would recognize her as a grown woman. Then he remembered her flaming-red hair, and knew he would recognize her at a hundred yards.

★　★　★

'Well, old pal, you're making good time.'

Grimm made the observation as they drew into the small town that, according to the sign they had just passed, proclaimed itself as Gulch City. The animal was indifferent to the praise, just kept a tired head low and headed for the livery stable to which his master was gently guiding him.

Suddenly there was a bang, and a machine trundled out of one of the alleys. Grimm steadied his startled horse and watched the noisy conveyance turn and disappear down the street, trailing a blue haze from its exhaust. One of those new-fangled automobiles he'd heard about. He waved his hand beneath his nose as the acrid smoke wafted their way.

The horse snuffled noisily, its wide eyes rolling in incomprehension. Grimm dropped down and sought to calm the beast.

'That's the stench of advancement, pal. Ain't nothing for you and me to do but get used to it.'

'Figure you got the right philosophy there, mister.'

Grimm turned to see a stocky, middle-aged fellow emerging from the stable.

'You the straw boss here?' the visitor asked.

The man toed at the straw on the ground. 'Straw boss?' he chuckled, rearranging the wad of tobacco in his mouth. 'Figure you can call me that.' He took a rag from his belt and began wiping his hands at the prospect of business. 'And what can I do for you, sir?'

'How far to Lobo Wells?'

The man looked at the setting sun. 'Ain't too far, maybe three hours.'

'That's what I figured.'

'But even if your hoss was Pegasus, you wouldn't get there before midnight.'

Grimm stroked the muzzle of his weary horse. 'Well, he's sure no Pegasus, and he's been on the trail since sun-up. Ain't right to push him further this day.'

He looked into the building, noted

the stalls and the relatively clean floor, and rated the place adequate. His mount merited reasonable accommodation, especially after the privations of the previous stop-over.

'You can quarter the horse overnight?'

'My pleasure, sir.'

'I'll give him a taste of water first. Then he needs a gentle rub-down and food. And after that, more water.'

While the ostler went to fill a pail, Grimm heaved off the saddle. On the man's return he allowed the animal to wash the dust down its throat, then he handed over the reins.

'Meantimes, can you recommend a hotel?'

'No need to — only one in town. Down the drag a pace. Can't miss it.'

His business concluded at the livery stable, Grimm registered at the hotel. Up in his room, he threw water over his face from a bowl on the dresser. As he towelled himself, he caught sight of his face in the mirror. It wasn't so much the stubble over the lined features that caught his attention, but the hair nearly down to his collar.

'Judas Priest, can't go walking into no church looking like that,' he mused, pulling at the matted grey strands. 'And I figure there won't be much time in the morning to get myself shorn.'

Downstairs, the desk-clerk directed him to the town's sole barbershop.

'If you hurry, you might just catch him before he closes.'

* * *

He did get there in time, but there was a customer ahead of him and the fellow was just settling into the chair as Grimm entered. Realizing he would be there for a spell, Grimm took a seat to wait, filled his pipe and looked around. There was a much-thumbed newspaper on a table at his side. He picked it up and casually flicked through the pages. Mainly local stuff, of no interest to him.

But then his eye was caught by a

picture of a new multiple-fire gun. It was under the heading of 'Science News', and described how the weapons were being drastically improved. Apparently the Gatling gun, which he'd once seen in action was now out-of-date. He had been amazed at the performance of that weapon at the time, and couldn't imagine how it could possibly be superseded.

Progress again, he mused to himself. Like that damn, choking automobile contraption. He stuck his thumb in the pipe-bowl to firm up the smouldering tobacco, and resumed his reading of progress in the big yonder. An American inventor had made what was called a 'telephonic transmission' by which actual speech travelled down a cable to a distant listener. Just like the telegraph — but with voices! Hell, what was the world coming to?

With another shake of his head, he closed the paper and returned it to the table. But as he did so a headline on the back page caught his eye:

He picked it up again.

'Well, doggone,' he breathed, as he read the details. The piece recorded the death of one Lee Hammersley, bounty-hunter. Lee Hammersley, his old rival! The story told how the fellow had succumbed to some illness in an out-of-the way sanatorium.

'So the crazy galoot has finally bought it,' he mused. 'Huh, the way he operated it's a wonder he made it this far. Died in his bed, too. Who'd a-thought young Lee would have gone that way?' For a moment he reminisced on the times their paths had crossed, and he smiled when he recalled how in their early days he had beaten the young hothead to the James gang.[1]

Hammersley had been maybe five

---

[1] The part Grimm played in bringing the James saga to an end is told in *Dollars for the Reaper*.

years younger than Grimm, but age had treated the fellow kindly, so, without Grimm's age-creased visage, he had an appearance at least a dozen years younger. They had been different in temperament, too. To Grimm, bounty-hunting was just a job. The lack of official law on the Frontier made the activity a necessity, if the more extreme renegades were to be curbed. But to Hammersley, it had been more akin to a sport.

And it always irked the younger man that in the game Grimm had a greater kill rate — but that was simply how things panned out, and why the label 'Reaper' had been slapped on him by some newspaper phrase-maker. Grimm was not averse to planting a guy, but he always gave the fellow a chance if he could. Hammersley never acknowledged his quarry as a human being, and proudly subscribed to the credo of 'one shot, one kill'. Grimm didn't know how many miscreants he himself had despatched — it was of no importance

— but the vain Hammersley kept records and newspaper cuttings of his own operations.

Grimm smiled ruefully as he cast a final eye over the piece. Well, Lee, old chum, this is one newspaper cutting you *won't* see. He folded up the paper and returned it to the table.

The paper had been right about one thing: things were changing. Horseless carriages. Machine-guns. He added these things to others in his own experience: telegraph wires snaking all over the country, new law-enforcement agencies like state police opening up. With such developments, it was clear that the need for unofficial operators, such as bounty-hunters, to fill in the cracks would lessen. Maybe young Lee had left the stage at an appropriate time, albeit inadvertently. And maybe it was time for Grimm to do so, too.

He was old. So was his horse. And, judging by all the fancy technical advancements going on, his very guns belonged in a museum. Maybe the finger had moved its full distance round the clock for him.

He thought of his funds, or rather, his lack of them. He contemplated his situation: at his time of life, it was all he could do to pull five hundred dollars together to offer as a wedding present. Judas Priest, that was no achievement! Where had it all gone? He'd never been one to live high on the hog. Born a Scot, there had been no squandering. But the way of things was, you made a grand here, maybe two grand there, then nothing for months and months. Earnings just went on living and horse-feed.

He'd got some bonds and certificates lying in some distant bank. But there wasn't much; and he couldn't even remember the name of the bank. Maybe if he cashed them, there would be enough to cover him for a few years. He rubbed a swollen knuckle against his gnarled cheek. Then again, how many years had he got? He'd never really thought about such matters. OK, maybe the time to call it a day was in sight. Yes. But not just yet.

He looked up and noted that the barber was getting near to the end of his shearing. He dismissed the matter of his late one-time rival, and drew on his pipe. But his mind insisted on forcing remembrances.

The two bounty-chasers had been as different as chalk and cheese. Grimm sought recreation in genteel pursuits, reading and such. Lee's good times were women and cards. Along with their different dispositions, their rivalry meant they didn't cotton to each other's company.

On the other hand, they were similar in some ways. They both practised their gun-skills regularly. And neither of them drank in any quantity. For Grimm, it was a matter of being professional. The occasional shot of rye or glass of beer was OK — in fact, booze was healthier than water in some towns — but no more. One needed a clear head when on duty, and a bounty-chaser was never off duty. For Lee's part, he didn't need alcohol; the job itself was intoxicating enough.

'Ready, sir.'

The voice shook him from his reverie, and he looked up to see the barber's chair vacant. The man shook hanks of shorn hair from his white sheet and indicated for his new customer to take his place.

'Got a wedding on tomorrow, so I want neat hair,' Grimm explained. 'Give me a shave, too. In case I ain't got time in the morning.'

'Ah, sir's getting married tomorrow.'

Grimm shook his head as he dropped into the chair and closed his eyes. 'Do me a favour!'

4

While Grimm was settling into his supper at the hotel, not too far away a young couple were also thinking of their evening meal.

Standing alone in the unsettled country, a few miles west of town, was a house of solid construction. Nearby were a small barn and a few outbuildings, and a couple of Jersey cows in a pen. In the yard a young woman on a stool was pulling at the teats of a goat while a young man watched her.

'Ready for supper?' she asked.

'You bet, Liz,' he responded, with relish.

'Won't be long now.'

He waited until the pail was full, and took it into the outhouse where the cheese was made. He emptied its contents into an airtight container.

'I keep thinking,' he said on his

return, when he handed her the pail, 'we can't live for ever on selling goats' milk and cheese.'

'Yes we can,' she replied, as she settled the bucket under another goat and resumed her task. 'Before Pa died, he'd paid off the mortgage on this place so there are no bills to pay. We supply most of our own food. And the money from milk and cheese provides cash for whatever else we need. Granted it's not much, but we get through each week without being beholden to anybody. That's something to be grateful for.'

'Yeah, what you say is true. But like I keep telling you, a guy needs to bring his own money into the household. He wants to be able to buy pretty things from town for his woman, with his own money.' He put his hands on her shoulders and whispered in her ear. 'Besides, we're going to get married one day, aren't we?'

She chuckled. 'I sure hope so, young man. And soon, too, I hope. We got to do something to stop those biddies in town tutting about our living together without the church's blessing.'

'And that means,' he went on, 'there'll be children one day, the Good Lord willing. Then we'll *really* need a wage coming in.'

'Don't keep fretting so. I'm sorry your working for the Big M fell through, but something will turn up.'

'I don't know, Liz. What with that and the other local outfits laying off men for the season, there's no work for an honest pair of hands.'

'Something will turn up,' she repeated.

'No. The only way I'll get work is by moving upcountry. I hear the spreads in the northern counties are expanding. Using the new railroad up there, they're beginning to ship beef out to Chicago. Could be boom times.'

'I can't leave this place. It's all I've got.'

'I know. I'd have to travel up there by myself. But I don't like leaving you. Lizzie.'

She looked up from her chores and

smiled. 'Why not? We trust each other, don't we?'

He bent down and nuzzled her hair. 'It's not that, Liz. It's just that I don't want to leave you. You're the best thing that's happened to me.'

'Well don't act so chagrined. Anyway, nearly time for supper. You'll feel better with a full belly.'

'Food,' he declared. 'That reminds me: I'll feed the horses.'

He crossed to the barn. There were two horses: his own mount, and the draught-horse Liz used to pull the wagon when she delivered the milk and cheese.

A quarter of an hour later, with the milking completed and the horses fed, the couple were in the house seated at the dinner-table. Around them the paraphernalia cluttering the interior reflected the choices of now-gone parents. The main kerosene lamp was set in a chipped Chinese vase; stuffed birds sat immobile under glass domes; an unused Bible lay on a shelf.

Among the more utilitarian items of the inherited bric-à-brac was a longcase clock. Tall against the wall, it gave out a dignified chime causing the girl to glance up from her meal. Almost absent-mindedly, she noted the time indicated by the fingers against the elegant Roman numerals, not realizing that she would have cause to remember the hour for a long, long time to come.

'How's your ma?' she asked.

'You know. Same as ever.'

'I've told you before, she could sell up her place and come and live with us.'

The man smiled. 'And *I*'ve told you before she values her independence. She — '

He got no further. The front door crashed open to reveal an ox of a man standing in the door-frame.

Within a second, the side door burst open likewise.

The young man leapt up from the table and grabbed the girl. 'Get behind me, Liz!'

'Liz? Cute name.' The speaker was an

elegantly dressed fellow, who appeared as the human battering-ram stepped aside to allow him clear entry. 'Close the door, Gaff.'

'Leave her out of this,' the young man said, his arms splayed out seeking to protect the girl now behind him.

As the door crashed shut behind him, the elegant one advanced, pulling at his gun. He shook it contemplatively and glanced around.

'So, this is where you live. Must say, sure is cosy.'

Then the side door slammed to, and the girl turned to see another two men advancing from that direction. She looked back at the pair approaching from the front.

'You know these men?' she said, her voice a mixture of fear and indignation. 'Who are they?'

Her partner ignored the question. 'What do you want?' he demanded of the intruders.

'You know too much,' the elegant one said.

'You got no worries on that score.

You know I'll never spill.'

'Who *are* these men?' the girl repeated.

'See,' her companion said, in an effort to make his point. 'Even Liz don't know who you are. I've told nobody. Nor will I. I got more sense.'

The other shook his head. 'I need some insurance, my friend. See, just your word alone ain't good enough.'

'Don't harm Liz. Leave her be. She don't know nothing.'

'Shall we kill 'em, boss?' the ox suggested in anticipation.

'Don't be a fool, Gaff. Odds are somebody will have noticed us leaving town and pegged our faces. No, we gotta be more subtle.' He gestured to one of the pair at the side, a young, long-necked fellow. 'Fan-Tan, you hold the girl. You other two, grab the brush-popper.'

For a moment there was scuffling while his orders were effected. Then he up-ended the table, china shattering as it hit the boards. He contemplated the young man, whose arms were now pinioned, before him.

Momentarily he rubbed the knuckles of his balled, black-gloved fist — then snapped the fist forward. The young man tried to ride with the punch but, constrained firmly by strong hands, there was not much he could do, and his head yanked back.

The girl writhed and tried to scream, but her mouth was clamped tight by the man called Fan-Tan.

'This is just a sample of what you'll get if you talk,' the attacker growled. And his fist smashed into the man's stomach. A cluster of solid punches to the head and midriff, and the victim hung limply between the two men.

Leather-clad hands grabbed the man's hair and yanked up his head. Blood was coming from his mouth and nostrils.

'Look at me, you bastard,' his attacker snarled. 'I want you to see who's doing this to you.' Then his fist snapped the man's head back again.

With yet another fist into his stomach, the man tried to suck in air, but a further two shots to the head put him out and once more he hung like a sack.

The big man looked back, noting a pan of water near the sink. 'Shall I bring him to with a dousing, boss?'

'No,' the ringleader said. 'That'll do for Lesson One.' Slowly he removed his gloves. 'Now for Lesson Two.'

He looked across at the girl. 'Get the woman down. Hold her on the floor.'

'Be a pleasure, boss.'

'Scream all you like, missus,' the chief murmured, putting his gloves aside. 'Ain't nobody gonna hear you out here. And when your boyfriend comes to, tell him there'll be more of this — in fact, worse than this — if he shoots off his mouth.'

And the thick stubs of his fingers ripped away at the front of her dress.

5

The next day, Jonathan Grimm stood at the entrance to the small church with Sarah, her hand lightly on his arm. She bore a small bouquet, and her face was hidden by a delicate veil. In contrast to the vision by his side, he was still in his trail-gear. He had only just made it, having had time merely to splash some water over his face and comb his trimmed hair.

The young groom, Frank, decked in new black clothes, stood at the altar looking pleased but awkward.

As the couple made their way down the aisle, memories of Grimm's own wedding flooded back. His darling Kate . . . [1] But such thoughts disappeared as

---

[1] Grimm's early married days and the passing of his wife are related in *Comes the Reaper*.

he and Sarah reached the altar, and the minister waved his finger for the participants to take their correct positions.

'Who giveth this woman to be married to this man?' he asked, in the sing-song voice unique to those of his calling.

It took Grimm a few seconds to remember his role; he cleared his throat and grunted, 'Er, I do.'

The traditional words were exchanged.

'You may kiss the bride.'

Frank gawkily complied, eliciting a chorus of sentimental sighs from the ladies in the congregation. Then, to the accompaniment of an organ, the party filed into the vestry for the signings. That done, the couple returned to the church proper. As they turned to walk up the aisle, Sarah glanced back and returned Grimm's wink with a smile.

God, she looked beautiful. The tousle-headed little urchin he remembered had become a goddess.

Outside, the sun shone on the happy

couple as they wove bent-headed under a shower of confetti. Finally, everybody made their way past the tombstones, down the hill and through the town to the Stanhope homestead where tables bedecked with food and drink awaited.

Shyly silent amid the noise, the bride and groom took their seats at the head of the table. Grimm was guided to a seat near the couple, alongside Hester, Sarah's mother.

Feeling like a fish out of water, he looked around, exchanging smiles with the unfamiliar, well-scrubbed faces of the gathering.

After a while, Hester leaned over to him and held his hand. 'I think it is appropriate that you should say something, Jonathan,' she whispered.

He squirmed in his chair, suddenly feeling now as awkward as the groom had been earlier. He harrumphed, and pretended to dust down his jacket, while his brain hunted for words. Then he stood and rapped the table.

'Folks, I'm told it's incumbent upon

me that I should say a few words at this juncture, so if you will indulge me . . . '

He cleared his throat again as his brain raced. Then: 'I don't know if you know, but our beautiful bride and I go back a long way. There was a time when she sat on my tow-horse. I think you'd be about ten, wouldn't you, honey?' He looked her way, and she nodded a smile.

'Well, I tell you, folks,' he continued, 'she stuck to me like a goddamn saddle-burr — and she was just as sure-fire irritating. Ornery, don't come into it. But we went through some scrapes together, and I got used to her ways, and in time I have to admit I didn't mind the red-haired saddle-burr sticking to me. You can see how pretty she is now. Well, she was pretty in her own way then, too — that is, when I could get her to clean the trail-muck off her little face.'

The audience chuckled with his attempt at humour, boosting his confidence. 'She used to ask me a heap of darn questions, like I guess kids do,' he went on. 'She might not remember this, but one question she asked me — was I rich?'

He raised his arms and looked over his bedraggled trail-clothes. 'I tell you, folks, what a question! But, truth be said, by then I'd fallen under her spell, and so I told her 'I ain't rich in terms of the folding stuff, honey — but with you in my life, I'm as wealthy as a king'.'

He looked at her again. 'And I'm telling you, folks, if she asked the same question today, I would give the same reply. The privilege of knowing our Sarah here makes me a rich man indeed.'

He picked up his glass. 'So, ladies and gentlemen, I beg you to stand and raise your glasses.' When the assembly did as they were bid, he raised his own glass higher. 'To the hearth and home — and may our young, newly-wed couple Frank and Sarah, have many years enjoying them.'

Then he sat down, hoping his

contribution, although short, was at least deemed sweet.

After a few more toasts and speeches, wedding gifts were presented.

Grimm handed an envelope to Sarah. 'I'd hoped it would be more,' he said, 'but there were snags.'

'Hoped it would be more!' Sarah exclaimed, when she had flicked through the bills. 'This is a *fortune*. Look, Frank!'

Unlike his wife, her husband took the money out and counted it. 'Five hundred! Gee, I don't know what to say, Mr Grimm. 'Thanks' doesn't seem good enough.'

'Just have a good and happy life,' Grimm replied, smiling. 'That'll be thanks enough.'

'Look, Ma,' Sarah said, pointing to the money in Frank's hand. 'Present from Mr Grimm.'

Hester looked across and raised her eyebrows, reflecting amazement at the wad; then she smiled in happiness for her daughter.

The subsequent meal was taken leisurely amid drink, chatter and laughter. Then a couple of old-timers struck up with fiddles. After the newly-weds had made a circuit alone, others joined them.

Hester took Grimm's arm. 'Let's you and me trip the light fantastic.'

'Dancing is one of the many social skills I never acquired,' he said. 'I would trip all right. Probably fantastically, too.'

But she wouldn't take no for an answer, and pulled the reluctant man into the throng. She guided his right hand around her waist and took his left. He proceeded to move — as lightly on his feet as a drunken sailor.

'It's been a long time since I had a man's arm about me,' she whispered.

He harrumphed and tried to concentrate on where his recalcitrant feet were supposed to go.

'There you are,' she said, after a couple of numbers. 'A veritable waltz king.'

'Yeah,' he grunted, 'and hogs fly.'

She took him aside after a while. 'Come, I'd like you to meet the boys.'

The 'boys' were her two brothers, Sam and Leroy, and three of their buddies. Grimm joined them at the beer-barrel. They replenished their glasses and found a stretch of grass where they could sprawl, talk and watch proceedings.

They were eager to find out more about the mysterious stranger. For instance, what was his connection to Sarah?

'I knew her ma and pa,' he said. 'There were problems. She was a young, lost kid, and it fell that I took her under my wing for a spell.'

Her being a young, lost kid was true, but the bit about taking her under his wing was a euphemism, for conversational purposes. The truth was more that circumstances had thrust her upon him, unwanted. At least, initially. She had been in the way, and caused him a heap of trouble. His liking for her had taken a long time in coming. But when it came, it made for an emotional wrench when he had finally found her a permanent home with the Stanhopes.

'And what happened?'

'Fact is, I didn't have a woman and in my line of work there's no opportunity for looking after a kid.'

'And what is your line of work?'

'I travel.'

'Doing what?'

'Providing services.'

He felt naked without his guns. Normally he was never without them, but he had deemed them inappropriate attire for a wedding. Otherwise, if he had worn them, his questioners might have noted the well-used appearance of the gun handles and might have guessed something about the nature of the 'services' he provided.

He parried further questions by asking them how they got by. Leroy was a blacksmith. The others were home-steaders and the like. He could have guessed, but had only asked in order to switch the conversation.

'Excuse me, gents,' he said, indicating his empty glass. 'Time for another.'

He'd just topped the glass when he felt a hand on his arm. It was Sarah.

'I'm so glad you could make it, Mr Grimm.'

'Nearly didn't.'

'Come, let's talk.'

She took his arm and they found a quiet place at the nearly vacant table.

'Now, tell me, what have you been doing?'

'You know what I've been doing. And cut that 'Mr Grimm' stuff. You're old enough, and we're close enough for you to call me Jonathan, young lady.'

She shook her head and smiled. 'You'll always be Mr Grimm to me.'

Their arms still linked, she cosied up him. 'You know, I was not much more than an infant the last time I saw you.'

He nodded at the remembrance of the little girl standing on the porch, clutching a ragdoll.

'Even now, still know little about

you,' she went on.

'Ain't much to know.'

'Oh, there's a lot I want to know.'

'Such as?'

She waggled her head as she thought. 'Many things. Well, for instance, do you have a wife?'

He shook his head.

'Has there ever been a woman in your life?'

'Oh, yes. I was married. Guess I wasn't much older than you at the time.'

'What happened?'

'She passed away.'

'I'm sorry to hear that. I never knew.'

As she spoke, Frank joined them.

'Hey, do I have cause to feel jealous?' the groom said, histrionically nodding to their locked arms.

'Yes,' Grimm said. 'You've got a beautiful gal here.'

'I sure have,' Frank grinned. 'If you'll excuse us, Mr Grimm.' And he grabbed his new wife. 'Come, time for another jig.'

'We must speak again,' Sarah said, as she was dragged once more to the dancing. 'There is *still* a lot to talk about.'

He watched the happy couple for a moment, then returned to join Hester's brothers on the grass.

It was a sunny day. The members of the group were relaxing, enjoying the atmosphere and each other's company, and chatting about the daily problems of eking out a living on the land.

After a while, Sam mooted, 'Say, fellers. Let's slip away to The Golden Dollar for a spell. We won't be missed.'

'The Golden Dollar?' Grimm queried.

'Yeah, its our regular watering-hole in town.'

'Won't Hester mind?' Grimm wondered.

'No. She knows our harmless habits. None of us are drunks. Anyways, it won't be for long. Be a break.'

'Sounds fine,' Grimm said. 'I look forward to it. I'll just let her know where I'm going.'

The others excused themselves from their spouses, fixed up a pair of horses to a wagon, and the group were soon trundling along the trail.

6

It was only a fifteen-minute run into town.

The Golden Dollar fitted the pattern of Frontier parlours. An imposing false-front with a grandiose title and a less than grandiose interior. The habit of drinking had never latched itself on Grimm, but he was no stranger to saloons. A goodly portion of his business was conducted in such places.

By the bonhomie with which the gang was greeted, it was plain the men were not unknown in the place.

'I allus wondered what you lot looked like,' the barman said, surveying the well-scrubbed faces of Leroy and Sam before he splashed beer into glasses.

'What you mean, Tel?' Leroy asked.

'Ain't never seen you without muck on your mugs. Now I can see your features.' He cast a glance around them as he placed the overflowing glasses on the counter. 'Mind, now I can get a good look at your faces, I think I prefer them covered up.'

'Watch it, pal,' Sam responded with a grin. 'Or somebody ain't gonna get a free drink.'

'Fancy duds, too,' the barman continued.

Sam explained about the wedding, as he took money from his pocket. 'And take one for yourself,' he added. 'You lippy critter.'

They took their drinks to a table and, calling for a deck of cards, began a small-stake game of poker.

After a while, Leroy took a watch from his vest.

'Time we were getting back,' he said. 'Otherwise we'll be stretching our luck.'

'Time for a couple more rounds,' Sam said, heading for the bar. He'd just placed his order and passed over the brimming glasses when a waddy burst through the batwings.

'There's a ruckus going on in the main drag.'

'What kinda ruckus?' someone shouted. 'Looks like there's gonna be gunplay.' There was a scramble for the door.

From the boardwalk, there was a clear prospect of the whole street. A block down, there were two guys squaring up to each other. The distance was too far for the revellers to hear the exact words of the exchange — but the raised tone was enough to indicate that, whatever the dispute was, it was serious.

Save for the gun-party applicants, the actual street was now empty, but they were not quite alone. Besides the crowd at the batwings, wide-eyed faces were visible at windows, and heads poked gingerly from alleyways.

Grimm felt less interest than the others. He'd seen it all before. He'd *done* it all before.

The voices of the two antagonists got louder as the sheriff emerged from his office. Hesitantly, he walked towards them.

Grimm watched the lawman. You're

doing it wrong, boy, he thought, as he assessed the situation from a distance. The state the game had reached — snarling, sweating, the reciprocal advances with trembling trigger fingers — you either dropped them both before they had a chance, or you kept out of it.

Out of instinct, his own hand moved, seeking the security of his gun, before he remembered it wasn't there.

Then the fireworks started. It happened so fast that nobody knew how many shots were fired — town gossip afterwards settled on four, but whatever the number was, it was enough to put two men flat on their backs. And the sheriff was one of them.

The survivor moved to his fallen adversary and kicked at the figure. Satisfied that the job was done, his brain moved to the next priority. He spun round, Joslyn pistol levelled, ready to challenge any intervention. Then he loped along the street, past the saloon, his gun waving from side to side, covering any eventuality. At the end of the drag, he threw himself on a horse and was gone.

'Must say, fellers, you lay on some good entertainment in this little old town of yours,' Grimm observed, pushing open the batwings. 'Sure glad you invited me to the shindig. Next round's mine, I believe.'

A couple in the party took up his offer, while the rest remained outside to monitor developments. Later, they returned and passed on their discoveries. No one knew who the combatants were, but it looked as though the sheriff would survive the superficial wound he had received.

An hour on, the revellers tumbled back in the wagon to make their return to the wedding feast, the shoot-out dominating the conversation all the way home.

★   ★   ★

It was around midnight. The guests had long since escorted Frank and Sarah away to see them ensconced in their honeymoon shack, and now the last of the revellers was finally gone. Grimm and Hester were seated before the fire in her house. He filled his pipe and lit it with a splint from the flames.

'That was some excitement in town today,' she said. 'Lobo Wells is such a quiet place normally.'

'You're the one who's had the busy day, ma'am. What with arranging the wedding and seeing folks are all right, and all.'

'I had a lot of help. Folk have been very helpful. Neighbours. The boys.' She thought for a moment and added, 'Such a pity Jim couldn't be here to see it.'

'Indeed, ma'am. But from what I've seen, Frank has the look of a regular guy. I figure he'll look after our Sarah. They got the makings of a happy couple.'

There was quiet until she said, 'It's good to see you again, Jonathan, after all these years.'

'Likewise, ma'am.'

'With you constantly on the move, Sarah was worried you wouldn't get the invitation in time.'

'Well, it found me, and everything worked out hunky-dory. Only snag, I was hoping to give her a bigger wedding present than I did.'

'What? You gave her a fortune.' Then she said, 'You know, considering all the years since you first rode in here, I still know so little about you.'

'Not much to know, ma'am.'

She studied him in the fire-glow. 'Well, let's start with the basics. Let me see. I detect a Southerner in your manner of speech. Georgia . . . Alabama, perhaps?'

He shook his head.

'Very well,' she continued. 'Louisiana?'

'You can keep on guessing, ma'am.'

'Keep on guessing? Why? You *do* come from the South, don't you?'

'No, ma'am.'

'Strange. There is an elegance to your

talk that a body doesn't hear in these parts. I would have sworn you were from somewhere south. Or maybe east?'

'Truth to tell, I was in the South long enough for some of their modalities to rub off on me.'

'Right, Mr Mystery Man. Where *do* you hail from?'

'Well,' he mused, 'even though I might sound like a true son of Dixie, there are some folks who can detect the remains of a Scots burr in my words, from time to time.'

She crossed to the fire and placed another log on it.

'Tell me about Scotland,' she said, and when she had returned to her seat, he noticed that she had sat a little closer to him.

'It's so long ago, I can barely remember it,' he replied. He remembered it very well, actually, but, not being a man given to conversation, he suddenly felt that he had been talking far too much. Besides, talking caused him to forget to enjoy his pipe.

'Is it all kilts and bagpipes?' she pressed.

He laughed. 'Heaven bless you, no!'

'Well?'

'If you insist, ma'am.' He closed his eyes; described the cottage in which he'd been born and bred; talked of raising sheep; told her of the heather-clad glens of summer, the snow-covered braes of winter.

When he opened his eyes, she had again moved a bit nearer.

'I must say, for a sheep-herder,' she said, 'you look at home on a horse.'

'Came to the States when I was a younker. Learned the trade on a horse ranch in New Mexico.'[1] He chuckled. 'Up till then, the only stock animals I knew anything about had been sheep. But the horse, now he's a whole different type of creature. I got to know the nature of the animal and its habits.

---

[1] See *Comes the Reaper* for his pre-bounty hunting days.

See, with sheep, apart from the lead ram and a few matriarchs, they're all the same. Just follow each other, like . . . well, like *sheep*, as you might say.'

He chuckled at his choice of phrase. 'But I discovered how each horse has its own character. Some are uppity, others have a sense of fun. And what I really like about the horse is that it's a plain-spoke animal. If he's a mean critter, he'll let you know from the outset. No shilly-shallying.' He studied a strand of smoke wisping upwards from his pipe-bowl. 'Yeah,' he concluded in a more serious tone, 'the horse has none of that deviousness which can characterize two-legged critters.'

He became aware of her inching a little closer, and he coughed to cover his embarrassment.

'Talking of horses, ma'am, I'll just give my own horse a last check before I turn in. If you'll excuse me, ma'am.'

★ ★ ★

When he returned, he was hoping that she had at last retired to leave him to his own devices, but there was a fresh cup of coffee and some cookies waiting for him by the fire.

'Have you ever thought of settling down, Jonathan?' she asked, as he munched reluctantly through one of the confections.

'Settling down?'

'Yes, while you still have time.'

'Time? I don't think of the passing of time in that way, ma'am. Just get on with my job and getting through the day.'

'Being realistic, there must come a time when a man has finally to put down roots. When the demands of his job become too much, and it's time to let the youngsters take over.'

He smiled. 'I don't work in a bank, Hester. There's no line of pen-pushing youngsters behind me, waiting to fill my shoes.'

'Even more reason. It would be my opinion that your job is somewhat more demanding than sitting at a desk in a bank, and all the more cause for you to think of retiring, putting your feet up.'

He chuckled. 'Putting my feet up? Where?'

She moved a little closer. 'Why, *here*.'

He stopped chuckling, and broke into a fit of coughing. He suddenly felt that, just like one of the sheep from his earlier days, of which he had recently spoken, he was being herded into a pen.

She patted him on the back as he spluttered.

'I'll be all right,' he said eventually, while as diplomatically as possible trying to put some distance between them. 'Some cookie went down the wrong way.'

His mind raced to try to find a different topic of conversation but, before he could, she continued, 'Yes, here. It would suit you fine here — here with me.'

He'd ridden a long way to meet an obligation, an obligation that he had been glad to meet. But he hadn't reckoned on getting himself involved in another set of obligations. And this biddy was hinting at — more than hinting at — a completely *new* set of obligations.

'Neither of us is a spring chicken,' she went on, 'but we do have *some* life left in us.'

He'd never thought of her in that way. She had been Jim's wife. And then, foster mother to Sarah. He had never thought of her as a *woman*. He looked at her in the firelight. There was no denying, she was still an attractive woman.

'No offence, ma'am, but I'm a permanent tumbleweed.'

'Even tumbleweeds fetch up somewhere eventually.'

He pondered on the analogy. Yeah, he thought, the wind blows 'em till they get stuck in some crevice. Well, the wind's not blowing me into a crevice. But these thoughts were too harsh to voice, so he said, 'What about Jim? *He* was your man.

'Yes. Was. But he's been gone some time. A respectable enough time for . . . '

She let the statement hang in the air unfinished, and he filled the space with, 'I knew him. Not for long, but long enough to see how you and he were together. It's my thinking that no one could take his place.'

'That's right. But you wouldn't be taking his place. You would be *you*. Jim has a place in my heart for ever. And you are *you*. There's space there for you, too, Jonathan.'

He harrumphed awkwardly. 'You don't know me. Not really.'

'And you don't know me. Not *really*.' She put her hand on his arm. 'But we're old enough to know that love doesn't come immediately, like in the storybooks. It starts with liking, and, if love comes, it comes gradually. On the other hand, if it doesn't come, a couple can still be a comfort to each other in their latter years. Life can still be pleasant.'

This line of thinking was way above

his head. He coughed. How could he put it in a tactful way?

'No offence, ma'am. You're a good-looking woman and all, but what you are suggesting is a big step. A mighty big step.'

'So?'

'Needs some thinking on.'

She smiled. 'I'll let you think about it.' She leant over and pecked his cheek. Then she stifled a yawn. 'It's been a busy day. Must lay my weary body down.'

She rose, checked the door and windows were locked, and disappeared down the passageway leading to the back.

'Goodnight,' he called, when it was clear she was finally retiring for the night. But she didn't reply. Hell, had he offended her? He hoped he hadn't said something to spoil the day. Staring blankly into the fire, he finished the cookies and coffee. Then he picked up the oil-lamp and walked slowly to the back.

Hester's room was marked by light and the sound of movement coming from it. He stepped into the one remaining room. His lamp showed a single bed; it was obviously Sarah's former room. But there were no sheets on the bed.

He put the lamp on a table and opened the door of the wardrobe. Inside, there were pillows and neatly stacked sheets. But the hinges had squeaked as he had swung open the door, eliciting a question from afar.

'What *are* you doing, Jonathan?'

'Just looking for stuff for the bed, ma'am.'

'No, no. Don't bother yourself: Come in here; it's cosier.'

'It was my understanding I would be sleeping in Sarah's old room, ma'am.'

'Tut, tut. Now I'm settled, you don't want me to disturb myself and start making up another bed, do you?'

'It's OK, ma'am. I can manage.'

'Don't be silly, Jonathan. And stop calling me 'ma'am'. My name is Hester, as you very well know. Now come in here, young man. It's nice and cosy. I won't bite.'

He stood for a while in the semi-darkness trying to work things out. But from behind him a voice, soft but insistent, purred: 'What *are* you doing?'

He sighed in resignation, picked up the lamp and crossed the passageway. In his long and tough life, he had been in a million tight spots. With his brains — or guns — or a mixture of both — he had managed to get out of each one of them. But tonight he had felt a lariat come snaking out of nowhere to land clear round his neck.

And he felt it being pulled tighter.

What's more, the old trooper hadn't a clue how to get out of it.

7

He turned over and was hit by a shaft of sunlight from the window stabbing through his eyelids. More pleasantly, the smell of fried bacon and eggs hit his nostrils. He breathed in deep. A delicious smell. His brain not yet working, he luxuriated in the aroma, musing on how long it had been since he'd had a proper, home-cooked meal.

Easing himself on to his back, he stretched his arms sideways — and became aware that his hands did not encounter edges to the bed! This was some bed; it was *huge*. Then it hit him: he was in a double bed! And as naked as the day he was born!

Sudden recollection of the previous night jerked his brain awake. His eyes snapped open and he rolled out of bed. His joints creaked as he got to his feet. He wrapped the eiderdown round his middle portions and tentatively staggered through the door. The stove was in use, with a simmering kettle and a couple of covered plates, but Hester was not to be seen. He advanced to the door.

She was washing clothes in a large bucket. She looked up and greeted him. 'Ha, Jonathan. Good to see you.'

'Er . . . morning, ma'am.'

She stopped her rubbing, and eyed him in a knowing way. 'Sleep well?'

'Er . . . like a babe, ma'am.'

'Your duds were sure in need of some cleaning.' She extracted a pair of long johns, held them up with suds dripping from her arms, and closely scrutinized them. 'Especially these. Who's been wearing them? Your horse?'

'You didn't have to, ma'am,' he said. He didn't mean it. He felt awkward having the woman being aware of his intimate body stains. He felt that his privacy had been invaded, and he would like to have said something to the effect of what right had the darned female got to meddle with his personal effects.

After an inspection, too detailed for his liking, of the underpants, she pegged them on the line alongside a dripping regiment of items from his wardrobe.

'Well, young man, by the time you get yourself freshened up, your breakfast will be ready. There's some hot water waiting in the kettle on the stove for your washing and necessaries.'

A minute later, he'd got his shaving-tackle ready and was looking into a mirror. He didn't care too much for what looked back at him. The dried skin of his face manifested a cobweb of fine criss-cross lines. His cheeks were sunken, giving him the gaunt aspect that accorded with the title of 'The Reaper', that unwanted label which had been tagged on him years ago by some fanciful newspaper-man. What the hell Hester saw in him, he didn't know.

He completed his ablutions and returned to the kitchen.

Hester placed before him a large platter stacked with the delicious food that had assailed his nostrils when he awoke.

'Gee,' he said, contemplating the feast. 'Bacon and eggs, hot water, feather bed. Where am I?'

She kissed his forehead. 'Plenty more where that came from, honey. Plenty more of *everything*.'

He was aware of the emphasis she had placed on the word 'everything'. Jeez, what was it with women?

'Are Sarah and Frank OK?' he asked, trying to change the subject, as he munched his way through the delicacies.

'Now, Jonathan, how do *I* know? Last night was their wedding night. Who's going to go a-knocking on their door over the next few days, asking them if they're all right?'

'Yeah, you're right.'

'I mean, we wouldn't have wanted anyone to come bursting in on us last night, would we?'

Jeez, he was trying his damnedest to

push the previous night's caperings to the back of his mind, but she kept reminding him. He wanted to say, 'It was a mistake, woman. A one-off,' but he couldn't form the words. He coughed awkwardly and stood up. 'Got a couple of carrots, ma'am?'

'My, my,' she said, that smile playing around her lips again. 'Are you never satisfied? I *am* learning about you. A man of big appetites in *all* directions. Didn't that breakfast fill you up?'

'It surely did, ma'am,' he said, dabbing his lips with a napkin, trying to hide his enthusiasm for getting out of the place. 'The carrots are for my horse.'

She laughed, and indicated a box. 'Help yourself.'

Outside, he breathed deeply of the fresh air, glad to be outside. There was a game going on indoors that he wasn't sure he understood — or cottoned to. He strode over to the small corral, opened the gate and entered. There was a time when he would have entered by climbing over the rail like everybody else; but for some years his ancient joints had said no to such impositions. Not to mention the extra strain to which they had been subjected the previous night.

Light cascaded into the stable as he opened the door.

'Morning, pal,' he said, approaching the stall.

The short ears of his horse, characteristic of the breed, swivelled in response to the familiar voice, and its broad head appeared over the rail. He gave the abundant mane a welcoming stroke, then slipped the latch and the animal trotted out into the morning sun.

As he watched him high-step round the perimeter, he was joined by Hester's brother Sam.

'Elegant mount you got there, Jonathan,' the man observed with a yawn.

'I thank you on his behalf,' Grimm said.

'Sure ain't seen an animal quite like it afore. A case in point, that fancy high-step trot. Like a circus animal. It been a show horse or something?'

'Naw, the gait is instinctive.'

Having worked the sleep out of its muscles, the animal halted at the fence near Grimm who stroked the attention-seeking nose that poked over the rail.

His companion studied the horse as it munched the carrot. 'Thought I knew my hosses, but that's a new one on me.'

'He's an Andalusian,' Grimm explained proudly. 'A mix of Arab and Spanish, just about the oldest hoss in the world.'

He parted with the remaining carrot, and was walking back to the house when he heard creakings behind him. Turning to see a wagon rolling up, he recognized Leroy and the three others from the previous day.

Howdies were exchanged, then Leroy said, 'Climb aboard, we're heading out to The Dollar again. You too, Jonathan.'

'Today's our regular day for some relaxation,' Sam explained.

'But we 'relaxed' yesterday,' Grimm said.

Hester had come to the door,

attracted by the noise and voices, and picked up on the conversation.

'They're all hard-working boys,' she said. 'Two days in one week, once in a blue moon, is not going to hurt anyone.'

'You sure you don't mind?' Grimm asked, praying that she didn't. Regular drinking and socializing was not his style, but in the present circumstances the notion had some appeal.

'Go on, join them,' Hester pressed. 'It's plain they enjoy your company, or they wouldn't be asking you. Anyway, you're one of the family now. They'd be offended if you refused. Enjoy yourself — and there'll be a hot meal waiting for you when you get back.'

Minutes later, Grimm was climbing aboard, with the worrying phrase 'you're one of the family now' ricocheting round his brain.

★   ★   ★

As they pushed through the batwings, the bartender Tel greeted them.

94

'Did you hear?' he said. 'It was Sonny Martin who got killed yesterday.'

The name obviously meant something to the others so Grimm asked, 'Who's he?'

'Lives — or lived — just out of town,' Leroy replied. 'Old man's Jed Martin. Got the biggest spread in the county.' Then, to the bartender: 'How's the sheriff, Tel?'

'He'll live to lock up a few more drunks.'

The bartender started pulling beers. 'And they've got a tag on his killer. A hardcase by the name of Black Ben Kelly.

'Never heard of him,' Sam commented.

The bartender relished his function as relayer of news. 'A no-good from Gulch City, so they're saying.'

Grimm remembered the name of the place, the small settlement he had passed through on his journey in.

'But you ain't heard the best part,' the bartender went on. 'Town council had an emergency meeting this morning. Issued their own dodger on him. They're putting up a grand for anybody who can bring him in. A grand!'

For the first time in two days, Grimm started getting really interested in what someone was saying.

Sam whistled. 'A grand! Hell, that's quite a sum to be offered on a private basis. Don't figure even the Justice Department would have stretched to that.'

'Yeah,' the bartender continued, 'Justice Department probably wouldn't have offered much above a few hundred dollars. But, with all the new businesses the council are expecting to attract in to town, they don't want the place to get a rep for lawlessness. Matter of local politics. So, they fixed up their own deal.'

'Besides,' Leroy added, 'as it was his son who got planted, I figure Old Man Martin will be chipping in a fair whack of that.'

After they'd spent their allotted time

in the saloon, the group crossed to the law office to see the poster before they left town. Their interest was merely to keep up with the excitement of the episode, the like of which the town had never known before. But Grimm's interest was a mite more professional.

BLACK BEN KELLY, the poster showed. WANTED FOR MURDER. It gave a height of five feet ten, and a weight of 180 pounds. It went on to describe a cast in the man's left eye.

When he'd verified the offer and noted the details, Grimm tried the door, but it was locked.

'Sheriff's in his sick bed,' a passer-by said.

'I know,' Grimm said. 'I was looking for his deputy.'

'Town don't run to a deputy.'

'What's your interest, Jonathan?' Sam asked.

Grimm tapped the figure of a grand on the poster. 'That's my interest.'

Sam considered the hard features staring back at him of the wanted man in the illustration. 'A feller fixing to rope that maverick would sure have to know what he was doing.'

'I know what I'm doing.'

Sam pondered on the enigmatic, but firmly given, response. And recalled their conversation of the previous day.

'This travelling you told us about yesterday,' he mused. 'These 'services' you provide . . . That mean you . . . you're a . . . '

The Reaper nodded in affirmation at the realization that was becoming explicit in the young man's eyes. 'That's right, my friend. Now, any idea how I can get in touch with this town council of yours?'

'Er . . . you'd best start by seeing the mayor. Come on, I'll take you.'

★ ★ ★

The mayor squinted through the smoke that curled up from the cigar between his lips.

'Normally, it would have been the

sheriff's responsibility to have took up the chase after the renegade. But, as you know, circumstances are that he couldn't. On top of that, it would take the Justice Department the best part of a week to get mobilized, with regards to some kind of reward arrangement. By then the trail would be cold.'

'It ain't exactly hot now,' Grimm countered.

'Anyways, that's why we're arranging our own deal.'

'How did you get the guy's picture so quick?' Grimm wanted to know. 'And how could you be so particular about all his physical details?'

'Sheriff recognized him from the regular documents he gets sent. Told us to look through the files in his office and we found an old dodger on the critter. Everything was on there.'

'This old dodger — what was the guy wanted for?'

The mayor took a document from his drawer. 'There: larceny with violence.'

Grimm absorbed the information.

The amount of detail compensated somewhat for the trail being almost a day old.

'Nothing about murder in his track record?' he asked.

'No, but, as they say, there's a first time for everything. And this is it.'

'Well, I'm your man, Mayor,' Grimm said. 'And I'm gonna want to move quick.' The mayor studied the man looming over him. Looked a mite long in the tooth to be lighting out after a young hardcase. But there was something about the fellow that obviated against making any comment.

'That's right,' Grimm said, reading the question in the mayor's eyes. 'Bounty-hunter. With a fully served apprenticeship. And, like I said, I need to move quick.'

'OK, I'll take your name, just for the record.' He made a note, and added, 'Well, we know he headed out on the northern trail. And already we know he went through Big Springs.'

'How come?'

'A local wagoner returned to town from Big Springs, learned of the trouble here and said he'd seen him out there.'

* * *

Back at the homestead, Hester's face reflected her anxiety on hearing of his plans. 'Do you have to?' she asked.

'It's my job, Hester,' Grimm said. 'You know that.'

'Well, if there's nothing I can say to stop you, I'll make you up some food.'

A quarter of an hour on, he was saddled up, his guns back in their rightful places, hanging from his hips.

Sarah had heard the news, and was standing close. 'Don't worry, Ma. Mr Grimm knows what he's doing.'

'Be seeing you, honey,' he said, clenching the girl's hand.

'You are coming back, aren't you?' Hester said.

He turned, and noted the sign of tears in her eyes. 'Sure thing, ma'am.' He had to come back to collect the bounty money, but he knew that wasn't what she meant.

Impulsively she pulled him to her, and kissed him fully on the mouth. 'You look after yourself, Jonathan Grimm. You hear?'

'I hear, ma'am.'

She wiped her eye with a knuckle. 'Not 'ma'am'; *Hester*.'

He bent down and awkwardly kissed her forehead. 'I'll take care, Hester.'

8

With his Andalusian bouncing under him, Jonathan Grimm felt at home once more. Although he had enjoyed attending Sarah's wedding, two days in one place with nothing to do but jaw and swill beer had already turned him fiddle-tooted. Not to mention the overtures from the lady of the house. Now he was not only back in action — but he also had a personal objective. A means for topping up Sarah's wedding present to a level more like the one he had first intended.

As his horse ate the miles, he pondered over the information he knew to aid him in his task: the man's name and appearance. Apart from the description on the folded dodger in his pocket, he had caught a glimpse of the man as he had run past the saloon, following the gundown. At the time,

Grimm hadn't seen the fellow as a potential quarry, and he'd had no need to note details. But his brain didn't need telling to make a record. It worked its own way naturally, perpetually logging details. And seeing a man in the flesh broadcasts other, subtler details. Such as the way a man moves. Everyone has their own distinctive way of moving. Not something you can easily put into words, more like a feeling. And having that kind of intuition helps in identifying a fellow at a distance — a distance too far to see the more obvious things, such as a scar or a cast in the eye.

And he knew two other things. The man carried a .44 Joslyn, not the most common of sidearms. That had been the thing he'd been waving about as he'd made his escape.

And the renegade rode a paint with a Mexican saddle. Hell, about the only thing the hunter *didn't* know about the critter was his mother's maiden name!

Moreover, he had an advantage. The

fellow wouldn't be figuring on being followed — or know who was following him. Lobo Wells was a one-horse town with one sheriff — and that sheriff was now flat on his back. With a population of dirt-farmers, the town would not have the resources to throw a posse together. The guy would know all that. That meant he would belt like the devil out of town, just to get clear, and then take it easy.

But the word 'easy' was not in the Reaper's vocabulary. As a catalogue of villains over the decades had learned to its cost, neither Grimm nor the horse under him was constitutionally built to take things easy.

Despite its name, Big Springs was even smaller than Lobo Wells. The kind of place where the comings and goings of strangers would be noticed. He rode between the handful of shacks that made up the settlement, and tethered the Andalusian outside the law office.

Normally, he only sought the help of regular law-officers as a last resort.

Badge-toters held a natural antipathy towards his kind. It was understandable. The kind of jack he could pull for doing the same job put their stipend in the shade. There again, their money was regular whereas he could spend months on a job and draw a blank. But not often.

However, he figured that the fact that his present quarry had downed a law-officer would sweeten matters. He was right. Not only was the sheriff sympathetic to his cause, but he had also seen the man. He had left town, continuing along the northern trail.

'How long since?'

'An hour, maybe two.'

Grimm nodded in satisfaction. The bozo had taken it *real* easy.

'Thanks, sheriff,' he said, when he had gleaned as much as he could.

★   ★   ★

His horse still fresh from the two-day rest-up, Grimm felt no qualms in continuing to ride fast to narrow the distance between him and his quarry, who was by all accounts now only a short distance ahead. His habit of watching the horizon while scanning the environs on either side of him came naturally. He always cut to a walk before topping high points. Then he would ascend real slow, studying the terrain about him before allowing himself to be outlined against the sky.

It was in this way that he found himself on tracks angling around a large rock. When he had turned past the towering obelisk, the trail fell away with a rocky incline to the left, flattening to a stretch of land to the right. The first thing he saw was a horse drinking at a trickle of a stream. It was a paint toting a Mexican saddle. Nearby its rider was sitting on a rock, swigging from his canteen.

Grimm reined in and tethered the Andalusian to a tree. He took his field glass from his saddlebag, slipped his head through the leather strap, and pulled his rifle from its scabbard. Making a final check that his horse couldn't be seen from below, he loped up the grade around the obelisk.

Slowly he worked his way along the slope, under cover of rocks and trees. When he was in reasonable range, he dropped behind a rock and took out his telescope. The fellow had now stoppered his canteen, and was building a smoke.

Even though the man had his back to him, he knew by the body shape that it was the man he had seen vamoosing hot-foot out of Lobo Wells, the man the poster described as Kelly.

The fellow was supposed to be over an hour ahead; he'd been taking it easier than even Grimm had imagined.

He took out his rifle, leant on the rock, and lined up. It was a tricky shot, even for the eagle-eyed bounty-hunter, but if the man didn't move, there would be no injury.

Bam!

The man dived to the ground as his

horse whinneyed and stomped. Looking every which way — the shot was still echoing around the landscape, making its source difficult to identify — the man grappled with his gun.

Locating Grimm, now heavy-footing down the slope, the man stared in disbelief at the Joslyn in his hand. Its trigger mechanism was shattered.

Grimm continued down the grade, repeatedly jacking in rounds and peppering the ground around the man.

'Don't move!' he boomed. 'I can place a shot as easily in your head as I did into your iron.'

'What is this?' the man yelled from his prone position, as Grimm neared.

'You know exactly what it is,' Grimm said, switching the rifle to his left hand and drawing his .44.

A minute later, the man was handcuffed.

'I don't see no badge,' he grunted as he watched Grimm prepare the horses. 'You ain't the law.'

'I work *with* the law.'

'That means only one thing: a bounty.'

'You catch on quick.'

'How did those small-town hicks happen to rope in a bounty-hunter so quick?'

'Just your bad luck I happened to be nearby with friends, when you started shooting up the town. Mighty rude of you to disturb our quiet drinking-session. You need a spell behind bars for that alone.'

He gestured for the man to get on his horse, but his captive remained motionless, mouthing, 'The bastard got what was coming to him.'

'Get one thing straight, pal — I don't wanna know.' Having dealt with scum all his working life, the one thing Grimm had learnt was that from the moment you got a bozo in gun-range you went deaf. They'd sell their grandmothers at wholesale price to be free of the shackles.

'Rights and wrongs ain't nothing to do with me,' he said. 'I'm just doing my job. Now get your ass in the saddle, and let's eat trail.'

★   ★   ★

It was late afternoon when he made it back to Big Springs. He rode the length of Main Street, looking for a boarding-house. It was too late to continue to Lobo Wells, and he didn't cotton to night-riding or bivouacking on the trail in the circumstances. Eventually he saw a sign proclaiming LODGING & BOARD, provided by its proprietor, a Mrs Cooper.

Inside the lobby, there was an odd smell to the place. But beggars can't be choosers.

'One room for two,' he said, when the woman announced she had a vacancy.

'I can oblige, sir, but it's only got one bed, a double.'

'That's OK, ma'am. My travelling-companion will be happy on the floor.'

'How long will you be staying for?'

'One night.' He figured he needed to give her some explanation, without

111

going into details, so he added, 'And just so you know what's going on, I'm a law officer transporting a prisoner. That present any difficulty for your establishment?'

The woman looked a little taken aback, then said, 'I guess not.' Then, as an afterthought, 'The charge will still be for two, what with breakfast and all.'

'Of course, ma'am. And we'll take our meals in our room, just so's we don't upset your other guests.'

Outside again, he looked down the road and noted a telegraph office. He got Kelly off his horse, took him across, and fixed him to a horse-rail.

The telegraph-operator was a small, pinch-faced man with a round, flat-topped cap. He took Grimm's dictation, then tapped: 'Have retrieved package. Should make Lobo Wells tomorrow. Grimm.'

'Will there be a reply?' he asked when he'd completed the transmission.

'Shouldn't be,' Grimm said. 'Maybe confirmation. In any event, I'm over at Mrs Cooper's.'

The telegraph-man eyed him. 'You like cats?'

'Haven't given the matter much thought. Why?'

'Makes no never-mind.'

★　★　★

He took Kelly in tow once more, and led him over to Mrs Cooper's establishment. As he entered, a couple cats were coming down the stairs. Another emerged from a doorway alongside, rubbing its back against the jamb. Another appeared from nowhere, and started pushing against his legs. Now he knew what the place smelled of; and remembered the telegraph-operator's enigmatic question.

An hour later, they were eating their meal in their upstairs room. Apart from the necessity of having to extract the occasional cat hair, the fare was reasonable. Grimm had unshackled Kelly so that he could eat. At the side of the room, with his gun handy, Grimm was taking his own food when there was a knock at the door.

It was the telegraph operator. 'Mr Grimm, I have a cable for you.'

Grimm took the paper and slipped the fellow a coin. 'Do not have courthouse in Lobo Wells,' the missive read. 'Take to Monument. Constable there has been notified to accept prisoner. Arrangements made for you to receive fee there.'

'Any reply?' the operator prompted.

Grimm wanted to reply and ask what the hell was going on. His contract was with the Lobo Wells Town Council. It was *their* job to get the critter to court. Then it occurred to him they would probably come back with a reply, pointing out they only had one sheriff and he was presently out of action, laid out on his back — blah, blah — so they weren't best equipped to accommodate the bozo or transport him — blah, blah.

He pondered on the implications. His mind had been adjusted to returning to Lobo Wells, along a trail with which he was now familiar. This was a new ball game.

'How far to Monument?' he asked the man.

'About forty miles.'

'Judas Priest,' he grunted, then capitulated. 'Tell 'em 'OK'.'

He passed over the fee for the new transmission, and returned to his meal. When they'd finished, he handcuffed Kelly once more to the bed-rail, and took the plates downstairs.

'Would like to light out early, ma'am,' he said.

'How early?'

'Sun-up.'

'No problem, sir. I'm an early bird myself.'

'Well, we'll turn in now. Goodnight, ma'am.'

He had gone no further than one step up the stairs when the tight-faced telegraph-operator came through the front entrance waving yet another piece of paper. He negotiated his way between the cats.

'Message, Mr Grimm.'

'Judas Priest, don't you ever close?' The man's pinched features tightened further. 'I live on the premises, sir. The gadget rings a bell when there's an incoming message.'

Grimm rolled his eyes. 'Huh, the advantages of modern technology. Very well.'

He took the paper. 'Package is to be delivered to me at Lobo Wells,' he read. 'This overrides previous messages. Will pay double original fee. Jed Martin.'

Hell's teeth, one thing he didn't cotton to was being monkeyed about! Even if somebody *was* stepping in with an offer of more mazuma.

'There is a reply,' he snapped. 'Got some paper?'

The man extricated a pad from his pocket, slipped the pencil from his ear and licked the end. 'Go ahead, sir.'

'To Jed Martin, Lobo Wells. My deal is with the town council. Only take their instructions.'

He yawned as he paid the fellow the

requisite money. Then, before he continued up the stairs, he touched the butt of his gun. 'And turn that damn bell off in the telegraph office, or I'll come across there and blow the frigger off the wall.'

On the landing, he nearly tripped over a cat. He watched the creature scatter, meowing its indignation with upright tail.

'The way they're going,' he grunted under his breath, 'one or two of these varmints is gonna get a bullet up the asshole, too.'

★ ★ ★

Before breakfast he went to the livery stable and tended to the horses' needs. Then he brought them round to a rail close to the boarding-house. He filled up the two canteens, and stashed the food prepared by the landlady into the saddle-bags. After coffee and a bite to eat, he paid the lady her due and bade her goodbye.

He tied Kelly to the paint, and made a final check of the horses. He had just put his foot in the stirrup when he heard a familiar whine.

'Mr Grimm, Mr Grimm!'

'Not another damn piece of paper!' he grunted, and turned to see the apprehensive face of the telegraph-operator.

'Afraid so, sir,' the man said, tentatively offering a familiar-looking chit. 'Only doing my job.'

'Some job — getting on folks' nerves all the time.'

Once more, Grimm fumbled for his glasses and peered through the lenses. 'Sorry you didn't settle for deal,' the telegraph read. 'Reconsider. I mean business. Jed Martin.'

'What's it say?' Kelly wanted to know.

'Seems somebody wants you real bad.'

'Any reply, sir?'

'Yeah. Just tell him: I mean business, too.'

9

Grimm rocked rhythmically to his horse's gait along the rutted trail to Monument. Two things annoyed him. First, the whole business of being diverted to Monument. This not only meant he was having to put in extra time to earn his money, but also meant more work for his aging horse. Although they had shared an active life together, both rider and mount were grey around the temples, and it was now becoming evident from their current caper that they both needed to slow down a pace.

The second thing that stuck in his craw was the constant complaining from Kelly behind him. He could handle the pleadings of innocence — that was all par for the course, and he could ignore them like water off a duck's back — but now the guy was gagging, and moaning about stomach pains.

'Listen,' he told him. 'I've heard it all before. Any excuse for getting off the horse, then looking for an opportunity to get the drop on me.'

'I ain't fooling, bounty. Must be something I ate.'

'That Mrs Cooper was a good cook, and we both ate the same. I'm OK.'

'Well, I ain't. Reckon I got some of them danged cat hairs lodged in my innards.'

Grimm ignored him, but a mile further on the fellow was still groaning.

'Cut your flapdoodling. We're due for a rest-up. When I can find a suitable place, you can go behind the bushes, if that's your trouble.'

'No, that ain't my trouble. Fact is, I always had stomach ailings. I need something to settle my guts.'

'Mighty odd you ain't mentioned it before.'

'Comes and goes. Sometimes it leaves me in peace for weeks. But anything can trigger it. Like I told you, I figure it's them cat hairs giving it some gyp.'

'You'll be all right with a coffee down you.' He looked at the sun. 'We'll be nooning in a spell, anyways.'

'Hell,' the man groaned, 'coffee only agitates it further. I need milk or tea.'

'Well, sorry, pal. Ain't got no milk or tea. If you care to look back, you'll notice I ain't hauling no chuck-wagon behind me.'

Except for the moaning, they proceeded in silence. Grimm was thinking of pulling in for a spell when they topped a rise to see a rolling plain stretching out before them. He drew rein to take in the prospect. Nothing for miles, save a speck beside the trail, which looked like some kind of habitation.

'There, that homestead,' Kelly said. 'They're sure to have milk. I'd deem it a favour if we can check if they got some to spare.'

'You've won,' Grimm muttered. 'Anything to shut you up.'

They ambled down the grade and eventually found themselves approaching a wooden shack. An elderly woman was in the foreyard, scattering feed to a flock of chickens. She looked up as they approached.

'Howdy, ma'am,' Grimm said. The chickens clucked and squawked indignantly as he reined in among them. 'My pardner here is in need of some milk. Something to do with his stomach. Could you oblige, ma'am?'

Silently, the woman appraised the couple. She saw the cuffs on Kelly, and backed away. 'Pardner? The man's tied to his horse. Sure don't look like your pardner to me.'

Grimm noted apprehension in her eyes. Figured she was alone. 'Don't worry, ma'am. I'm a lawman. He's my prisoner. So, if you could oblige — I'm willing to pay — and then we'll be on our way and out of your hair.'

She stood looking at the two of them. Then: 'Very well, I'll fetch some milk. Meantimes, you could water your horses if you've a mind.'

'Mighty kind, ma'am.'

The woman mounted the rickety steps back into the house while Grimm slid out of his saddle and helped his prisoner down.

'Just back off where I can see you,' he said, and proceeded to water the horses. When he had allowed the animals a few laps, he looked back at the shack for the woman, but there was no sign. Then he looked over to his prisoner, took off his hat and wiped sweat from his brow. He smoothed back his greying hair and was setting the hat back in place when something hard jabbed into his back.

'Don't move, mister, or you'll be gut-shot.'

He stiffened with what he figured was a gun-end jabbed hard against his spine. He hadn't heard the creaking steps at the front of the shack. The woman must have crept round the side of the building deliberately.

'What took you so long, Ma?' Kelly

grinned and passed behind Grimm, adding, 'Gimme the gun.'

The weapon moved against Grimm's spine as it changed hands. Huh, he thought, Kelly's mother lives on the Big Springs-Monument trail. *That* was a little item that hadn't been in the dossier. Still, he should have guessed something didn't smell right. Age does a lot to a man. Dulls his senses. And his common sense.

In the illumination shed by hindsight, Grimm saw what his common sense should have told him: the ploy about being ill; Kelly was on his home patch, it all fitted into place. Must have stopped at his ma's here on the way, too. And that would provide further explanation as to why the man hadn't covered as much ground as the Reaper had expected.

'That was sure white of you, Ma, not hollering out to me when you saw us approaching.'

'Used my brain, Benny,' she said. 'Didn't look right. Then I clapped eyes on those cuffs on my boy. That was enough for me.'

'Now take his guns,' Kelly went on, and jabbed Grimm with the rifle-end. 'And you — any funny business you get this.' He worked the weapon in a prodding circle round the man's back. 'Can't miss from here.'

'Now get the key to these damn cuffs, Ma,' he said when Grimm's two side arms were out of harm's way. 'In his left vest pocket.'

'I could shoot you here and now,' he continued, when he was freed. 'Be the end of my troubles.'

Grimm turned. 'No, it wouldn't. It would merely add to the manure you're already in.'

'Put your hands forward.'

Grimm remained unmoving.

Kelly grinned. 'Boot's on the other foot now, ain't it? Now, do as I say: put your hands forward. I only have to pull this trigger.'

When Grimm was handcuffed, Kelly walked to the fence and hurled the key into the scrub. Then he unhitched the Andalusian and hit its rump. As it scampered to freedom, he fired a shot above its head. Carrying a man like Grimm for years, the horse was no stranger to the sound of gunfire, but it could still be spooked by a slug zinging between its ears; and it was soon on its way towards the horizon.

Kelly rolled a cigarette and smoked it while he thought about his next move. Then he put his arm around his mother. 'I gotta move, Ma.'

'What shall I do with him?' she asked, nodding towards Grimm.

'He can walk back to town. It's only twenty miles.'

'In handcuffs?'

Kelly stamped out the cigarette, looked at the bounty-hunter and chuckled.

'Ain't your day, is it?'

He picked up Grimm's pair of guns. He only had a one-holster belt himself, so he chose one gun and slipped it into the sheath. He shucked the shells from the remaining weapon, and hurled that out into the scrub.

He looked back at the woman. 'And don't worry about being in trouble for helping me. The old buzzard told you wrong. He's not law. Just somebody who can't mind his own business. Sheriff can't have you for that.'

He clenched her hand.

'When will I see you again?' she asked.

'Sometime, Ma. You can be sure of that. But I can't make any promises about when, not while I'm in this stew. But I'll be back. Ain't I always?'

He drew the pistol and pointed it at the bounty-hunter. 'Now you, oldster. Hit the trail.'

Grimm said nothing and walked out of the yard. He started heading back to town, keeping one eye out for the Andalusian. When he had trudged a couple of hundred yards, he stopped and looked back. Kelly was now a spot in the distance in the other direction.

He quartered the four points of the

compass. Still no sign of his horse. He looked up at the setting sun and contemplated the twenty-mile walk, most of which would have to be done in the dark. He turned on his heel and headed back to the shack. He made for the scrub where the key had been thrown. He scratched around till it was too dark to see, then returned to the shack and lay on the boards of the veranda.

Hearing the creaking, the woman opened the door. 'He told you to go.'

'Ain't no way I'm walking back tonight, ma'am. If you don't want me here, figure you're gonna have to shoot me.'

The door closed, and he let his head fall back on to the woodwork. Minutes later, the door opened and the woman reappeared. Without a word she put a pillow under his head and laid a couple of homespun blankets over him.

'Night, ma'am,' he said, and lowered his head, wondering if sleep would come in such an awkward position.

It did come. Eventually.

* ★ ★ ★

He was woken by something pushing at him. He knew what it was before he opened his eyes: the touch of velvet flesh, the smell.

'Hey, feller,' he said, rolling over. 'You made it back.' He did his best to stroke his horse's muzzle with his handcuffed hands. 'You thinking the same as me?' he asked the animal, after a brief spell of mutual comforting. 'That we're a mite too wizened now to be on these kind of capers?'

He got to his feet, every muscle and joint in his body stiff. The first shafts of sunlight were cutting across the landscape. He made for the scrub and resumed his search for the key. In time he was joined by the woman. He looked at her questioningly.

'Don't worry,' she said. 'If I find it, I won't throw it away again.'

He shrugged and continued his search. Whether or not he believed her, there was nothing he could do about it.

Eventually it was she who found it. She raised it triumphantly, and walked over to him.

'Thanks, ma'am,' he said seconds later, rubbing his freed hands.

'Come and have some breakfast.'

'Obliged, ma'am. I'll join you when I've found my gun.'

★　★　★

Fifteen minutes later, he pushed away an emptied plate.

The woman was looking at him. 'My Ben's not a bad boy, really. Got off on the wrong foot, is all.'

Would a mother say anything less? Grimm thought; but he said nothing, and let her carry on.

'But he's paid for that, mister. Did his time.'

'What's he been doing since?'

'Working here and there.' By her demeanour, it didn't sound as though the infamous Black Ben Kelly had put his mother in the picture about his latest claim to fame — gunning someone down. 'Odd jobs, cowboying and stuff, that kind of thing.'

The circumstances were not fitting for Grimm to point out that, somewhere in the catalogue of his activities, her son had found time to kill a man. He just said, 'I appreciate the spot you've been in, ma'am. With your obligations to your son, and all. Only way out was for you to have shot me. Obliged that you didn't, ma'am.'

'I couldn't have shot you. And I couldn't have let you wander across open country with your hands shackled.'

'Thanks for your kindness. And thank you for the filling meal. Must be going.'

She followed him outside and watched him tending to his horse.

'What you gonna do now? Chase after him again?'

'You did your son proud, ma'am, delaying me like you did. He's been left ten hours or more. So, don't worry on that account. You think I stand a prayer in catching him with the head start that you've given him?'

'I did what I had to do. Like I've told you, he's not a bad boy, deep down.'

'If it's any consolation, ma'am, you're not adding much to his troubles by having helped me a mite. Fact is, there's going to be more than one on his trail. So you'll have to reconcile yourself to things. If it's not me, ma'am, it'll be someone else. But I'll promise you one thing: if I do catch up with him, I'll treat him civilized, bearing in mind that's the way you've treated me.'

10

Another day on, Grimm was still heading along the same trail. Although he had no guarantee he was on the right track, he had persevered. It was a well-rutted trail, and displayed a good deal of horse-droppings. But some recent leavings were from a grain-fed horse. Such a diet would not be usual for a horse from these parts, which were plentiful in summer grass. But, he guessed, Kelly's horse was a town animal, and grain-fed. It was a long shot, but the only one he had.

In the late afternoon, he came to a sod-roof farmhouse, a little distance off the trail. Espying a pump and trough, he wheeled his horse to the side and rode down the lane and through a break in the lodge-pole fence. Nearing the building, he could hear the grunt of pigs, the clucking of hens and an occasional hammer-blow coming from the back. As he drew rein near the pump, a young woman came to the door.

'Mind if I water my horse, ma'am?'

'Feel free. There's a pail yonder.'

'Obliged, ma'am.'

He swung down and collected the pail from a hook on the wall. As he worked the pump, he noticed a cigarette butt on the ground. The rounded ash was still intact. He scuffed it casually with his foot, and the fragile ash disintegrated. Couldn't have been there long; the slightest wind would have already dispersed the burnt residue.

'Rid far, mister?' A male voice.

Grimm turned to see a young man coming from the back of the building. The fellow had a hammer in one hand, and nails in the other.

'Lobo Wells.'

'Lobo Wells!' the woman exclaimed. 'Would you believe it? We hail From Lobo Wells, don't we, Matt?'

'A nice place to hail from, ma'am,' Grimm commented.

'Well, if you've come from Lobo Wells,' the man said, 'then, like your horse, you could do with refreshment, too. Coffee's on. I was just about to have a break from my chores.'

'That's mighty kind.'

When the Andalusian had finished drinking, Grimm half-hitched the reins to the fence and followed the couple inside. He took off his hat and followed the gesturing hand to a seat at the table.

'You seen a feller on a paint riding this way?' he asked, as he settled himself: 'Mexican rig?'

The man shook his head. 'No. Ain't seen hide nor hair of anyone for a couple of days.'

The visitor nodded, then thanked the woman when she placed steaming mugs before the two men.

'You say Lobo Wells,' the man said contemplatively, 'but you ain't local. Leastways, you ain't got the local way

135

of talking, and I don't recognize your face.'

'No, I ain't local. And as for my way of talking, figure that'll come from my being born in Scotland.'

'Can't detect any Jock in your voice, either.'

'Forty-odd years in God's Own Country have gotten rid of that.'

'Well, what brings you out this-aways?'

'I was honoured to be attending a wedding.'

'Would that be the Stanhope girl?' the woman asked.

'Sure would, ma'am.'

The look of mild surprise on Grimm's features prompted the husband to explain: 'My wife tries to keep up with things back there.'

'Yeah,' Grimm went on. 'The prettiest thing you ever did see.'

'Now, what's her name?' the woman mused.

'Sarah,' Grimm answered.

'Ha, yes, Sarah. Real pleasant girl, as I recall.'

'You folks get back to Lobo Wells

often then?' Grimm asked.

The woman looked in mock reproval at her husband. 'Not often enough for my liking. Lobo Wells is the nearest thing to what can be called civilization around here.'

The man threw a glance back at her. 'We've not been out here too long, and my dear wife still hankers for town life.'

Grimm took a sip of coffee and looked through his pockets. 'Say, you folks got a smoke? I've run out of makings.'

'I'm sorry, we don't smoke,' the man said.

Grimm nodded. He was trying another long shot.

'I thought so,' he said, a more serious tone entering his voice. 'Now, you say you ain't seen nobody for a long spell, but *somebody*'s been here recently. Very recently. There's a new cigarette butt out front.'

There was a pause and an exchange of glances between the couple. Then the woman said, 'Oh, tell him, Matt. The feller's genuine enough, knowing the Stanhopes and all.'

The man looked sheepish. 'Ain't that we make a practice of lying, mister. Just that we gotta be careful. We don't want to get mixed up in other folks' affairs, you understand.'

Grimm nodded. 'And?'

'Feller did stop by; watered his horse, as you've done. Mexican saddle and all.'

'This horse, it was a paint?'

'Yeah. Nice looking animal. Trouble was, it'd got a limp. Asked if he could exchange it, but we don't have any horse stock.'

A lame mount. That would explain how Grimm had managed to make up the time again.

'How long since?'

'Hour, maybe two.'

'Anything marked about the guy's features?'

The man shook his head, but his wife said. 'Got something wrong with his eye. His left eye.'

Grimm nodded. 'Which direction?'

'Towards Sundown, the next town out that-aways. But that ain't where he's headed. I took a look out that way sometime after he'd left. Saw him turn north of the trail.'

'Whereabouts?'

'About a mile further on. By a stand of yellow pine. You can't miss it.' Then he added, 'This feller, what do you want with him?'

'Got some business to transact.' Grimm picked up his hat and walked back to the door. 'Thanks for your hospitality, folks. And don't worry about your being open with me; you ain't interfering in nobody's affairs.'

★　★　★

Grimm had been thinking he'd lost his quarry, but now that he knew he was only a few hours behind the fellow, his spirits rose.

He turned off at the indicated point and worked his way through the trees.

Eventually, he emerged to find his passage barred by a stream. He reined in and considered the terrain that stretched beyond the rippling water. Healthy sward, reaching up to foothills. He squinted, quartering the scene methodically, and it wasn't long before his eyes, ageing but still retaining some keenness, could make out the faint sign of a track through the grass.

The bounty-hunter knew his trade. To the trained and experienced eye, the clues were everywhere. It was just a matter of listening, watching and reading.

He nudged his horse across the stream, and headed along the track. He could tell it had been recently made: the bent stalks of Indian basket-grass had not yet returned to their natural angle. Eventually, he came to an area of flattened grass marking a bivouac. The man had rested here a spell. He ground-tethered the Andalusian and, constantly studying the ground, Grimm walked along the track. Some distance on, he spied horse-droppings. He hunkered down and felt a ball of the stuff. Cold. He broke it open, sensing the vestiges of warmth remaining in its interior. Yes! Only an hour or two, at the most. The dung was mainly grass, but contained remnants of grain. That would fit the pattern, Kelly's horse having been grazing along the trail.

The bounty-hunter returned to the flattened grass area and thought on it. In summary, all the signs were that the rider ahead of him *was* Kelly and had passed by not too long ago. So far, so good.

But something was wrong. A man on the run wouldn't take a casual rest out in the open. The flattened grass had been formed to catch the eye of a pursuer, that was his guess. Further, a man on the run and away from a used trail would be alert to his mount leaving tell-tale droppings. He would try to hide them. Moreover, this track led up to the mountains, their white peaks scratching the distant sky. Unprovisioned and scantily clad, the man would be the seventh son of a jackass to fetch up deliberately in the mountains when the bitter night fell, even with his liberty at stake.

Grimm walked his own mount back to the stream and guessed the scenario. His man had come to the stream, crossed it, and put effort into making an obvious track and a bivouac area. Then he'd backtracked to the stream and proceeded along it. But which way? Probably not east, as that wound back towards town. A man on the run wouldn't take the risk. Unless he was a double-bluffer.

Discounting that notion, the tracker got back in the saddle and urged his horse along the shallow stream in a westerly direction, his eyes constantly scanning the bank looking for signs of exit. In time, he came to a rocky surface. He left the stream and dismounted again, this time allowing his horse to drink while he himself slow-footed across the gentle grade, constantly observing. A man might think he left no tracks on rock, but, if a horse had come this way, there would be scuff marks. So slight they might hardly be seen, and would certainly be weathered away within a day or so, however, if recently made, the marks would be discernible to a patient eye.

Now and again the Reaper crouched down to look. Eventually, his lips curved into a smile. Here and there, faint but unmistakable hoof scratches; and heavier on one side, the sign of a lame horse. So, *that* was the way he'd gone.

He returned to the stream and refilled his canteen from the clear water. He mounted and headed across the rocky surface.

Although Kelly was still way ahead, Grimm had two advantages over his quarry. First, the lame horse. That fact alone stacked the odds against the fugitive. But on top of them, Grimm was also an experienced tracker.

★ ★ ★

It was early evening when Grimm turned up into the foothills, threading his way between larches and yellow pine. The ground was now soft, the tracks easier to follow. Then, ahead, he spotted a line shack. It looked deserted. The man would be tired and cold, maybe low enough in spirits to chance using the accommodation if it was empty.

The Reaper backtracked till he was well out of sight of the building. He picketed his horse, then slowly worked his way upwards between the trees, so he could observe the place from cover. He stayed that way for a while, just watching. When he had concluded that, should Kelly be in there, he hadn't observed his pursuer, Grimm circled round to make his approach from the rear.

Then, his doubts were dispelled. There was a paint tethered in a lean-to; he knew he had reached the end of his journey. Taking out his Colt, the hunter went from cover to cover till he was near, then he loped to the building, careful not to disturb the resting animal. He listened for a spell. His hearing was less good these days, but he eventually picked up the regularity of breathing coming from inside. He stepped back, summoned up his strength, and slammed open the door with the bottom of his booted foot. Inside, the fatigued man was startled awake.

'Christ!' the renegade groaned, his tired brain trying to make sense of the ruckus. Then he saw the hunter and the levelled gun. '*You* again.' Within a few seconds he had composed himself and accepted the situation.

'I'll be obliged for the return of my gun,' Grimm said. 'Take it out with your left hand.'

When the gun was back in its proper holster, the Reaper re-shackled the man's wrists.

'How did you get back on my trail so fast?' Kelly wanted to know.

'Let's just say things panned out that way.'

The man suddenly looked concerned. 'You didn't hurt Ma?'

'Now, would I do anything to an innocent little old lady?'

Kelly looked around the dark, austere cabin setting. 'Figured it was still Frontier enough up here to give a man room to get lost in,' he grunted, wearily.

'Not with me on your tail, pilgrim.'

11

They came trailing out of the shimmering scrubland, two dust-grimed figures astride weary horses.

There was hardly anybody about as they turned into the main drag. Grimm steered the small train towards the nearest hitch-rail adjacent to an alley, and reined in. He negotiated his stiff body out of the saddle and tied the reins to the rail. He grunted as he worked his rheumatic shoulders and arms.

He was about to step on the boardwalk, when an explosion shattered the quietude and his horse slumped forward to its knees, then keeled over, knocking the Reaper to the ground, trapping his feet. Kelly's horse bucked, spilling its rider, whose hands were still fixed to the pommel.

As Grimm struggled to work his legs

free, another bullet whacked a chunk out of the boardwalk step close to his head. He heaved at the deadweight of the animal and managed to extricate his feet. Once clear, his movements were purely instinctive, honed by a lifetime's experience. The slugs coming over his shoulder meant the firer was behind him, so the boardwalk offered no protection. He scrambled to the nearest effective cover, the alley, wincing at the stabbing pain in one of his ankles — guns immediately drawn, head turned, eyes seeking the location of the shot.

He glanced at his downed horse — what could he do? — but as another bullet splintered wood inches away, he hurled himself further down the alley. At the end of the passage, yet another shot tore a painful furrow across his left shoulder. And that came from ahead.

Judas Priest! He was pincered — there was another bushwhacker covering the back of the building.

Ignoring the assorted pains, he

retraced his steps and smashed through a door part-way along the alley. There was an old couple huddled together, clearly distraught by the gunfire.

'Just keep out of the way, folks,' he said, 'and you'll be OK.'

Crossing the room to push through another doorway, he found himself inside some kind of clothes-store. As he took in the scene he felt his shoulder, and he winced noisily as his fingers explored the soreness. There was a counter behind which bolts of material reached for the ceiling in racks. More important, he noted, there was a door to the rear and, at the front, large display-windows from which he could be seen from the street.

He passed behind the counter, stepping over a broom, and picked up a chair, the back of which he rammed against the knob of the door. It wouldn't stop the fellow at the rear of the building, but at least he would hear the bozo coming. And then he returned to the front.

Somewhere out in the street a gun cracked, and the nearest window exploded, a cascade of glass segments and slivers crashing to the floor.

Grimm flattened himself against the wall. He thought fast. He crouched down and, taking off his hat to minimize his being a target, moved along the skirting, taking care to keep his head low and not to crunch glass underfoot. Reaching the further window, he stood up and hazarded a one-eyed look at the main drag. The critter was out there — but where? Hell, this cat-and-mouse game could go on all day.

He receded into the relative darkness of the interior and looked around. Further back stood a tailor's dummy, sporting a wide-brimmed hat decorated with flowers and a full-length bustled dress.

From behind the counter he collected the broom and laid it on the floor near the front. Then, maintaining a watch on the windows, he removed the headgear from the mannequin and

150

eased off the dress. He slipped his jacket over the dummy's shoulders, and placed his own hat on the faceless head.

Keeping low, he took his gun from its holster and inched the dummy closer to the remaining intact window. With the sun reflecting on the glass, he reckoned the mannequin would register more as a moving shape than a distinct figure. He was right.

The gun barked again, disintegrating the second window. Using the broom, he jabbed the back of the dummy so that it teetered, then toppled through the window-frame. Immediately, he sped across to the other window in time to see a figure rise from behind a barrel on the boardwalk. The man advanced confidently, throwing a succession of jack-levered shots at the downed dummy.

Grimm leapt into the frame. His first shot took the fellow in the shoulder. The man started awkwardly, his rifle raking crazily in the Reaper's direction. But the next slug from the .44 was a heart shot, and the fellow crashed to the boardwalk.

Grimm scanned up and down the street, then swung his rangy legs over the frame. He was about to step off the boardwalk, when he caught a reflection in a store window opposite. Silhouetted plainly against the sky was the second man with a rifle — now on the roof *above* and *behind* him. He drew his second gun and turned round. Both guns were pointing skywards as he stepped backwards off the boardwalk. And both guns were firing as he broke from the cover of the overhang.

The knees of the man on the roof crumpled — and he pitched forward. On the way down, he hit the overhang and bounced to the street. Judging by the right-angled twist of his head in its final position, if the Reaper's fusillade hadn't killed him, the fall had finished the job.

'What the hell's going on?'

Grimm whirled round. It was the sheriff on the other side of the street, a rifle in his hand.

'You tell me,' Grimm growled. 'It's your town. I've only just rode in.'

'Drop that gun,' the sheriff ordered.

Grimm looked along the rooftops, then up and down the street. Townsfolk were beginning to make tentative appearances.

'Not until I'm sure there's nobody else in this burgh of yours about to throw lead at me,' he grunted.

Still keeping vigil with both guns, he edged along the street to his grounded horse. The animal's head was transfixed in a grotesque attitude, still strung up by the reins tied to the rail. He made a final check for gunmen, then sheathed his pistols. He took the weight of his mount's head, cradling it gently, and pulled his knife. He slashed the leather strips; then tenderly lowered its head to the sand. The dark, long-lashed eyes were closed, and the hole visible through the mane at the back of the skull was testament to their never opening again.

Sickened by the realization, he stroked the neck of his beloved mount in contemplation for a moment, then rose and exhaled noisily — a sound reflecting his feelings at losing a long-time pal, but simultaneously indicating his resolve to do something about it.

He looked once more down the street. Nothing, save for a faint spot in the distance, a figure emerging from an alley. Grimm considered him briefly. The man looked towards him for a few moments, as though assessing the scene, then continued on his way in the opposite direction.

Grimm dismissed him as a local posing no threat, and looked the other way. That was more promising. There were three horses tethered at the end.

'They belong to those guys?' he rasped, drawing one of his guns and shucking the used cases.

'Guess so,' a bystander offered. 'They belong to a bunch of strangers who rode in about half an hour ago.'

Grimm extracted bullets from his belt and slipped them into the chamber.

'I can count three horses. That means there's one bastard still needs accounting for.'

He looked the other way and contemplated the distant figure once more. Was *that* him? But his question was answered when a bystander pointed in the opposite direction and shouted, 'Look, mister!'

Near the three horses, another fellow, this one with a rifle, had appeared out of an alley.

Grimm grunted in satisfaction. '*That*'s the bozo.' He sheathed the one gun and drew the other, glanced at the sheriff and jabbed a thumb towards his prisoner. 'I'd be obliged if you'd keep an eye on him, Sheriff. I got unfinished business.'

He started along the street, topping up the loads in his second weapon in a mechanical fashion, without even looking at it.

Seeing the lone man progressing

towards him, the man let fly with a shot from his rifle. Everybody in the street reacted by diving for cover.

That is, save one — the Reaper, who maintained his gait unflinchingly down the middle of the street, his eyes slitted with determination.

His quarry made two mistakes. At that distance, he stood a better chance with his rifle against his adversary. He had time to reload and take several considered shots before the advancing man would be in realistic range with mere handguns. But there was something about the looming, ominous figure that sent a shudder through his body and, instead of reloading, the man dropped the rifle, grabbed at his horse and struck out of town.

That was his second mistake — to leave the horses at the rail.

As Grimm approached the animals — a chestnut Tennessee and an awkward-looking palomino — he instinctively gave them the once-over. The Tennessee was larger, and had the elegance of his breeds; a less experienced man might have gone for it. But Grimm was not seeking a comfortable ride, which is what the breed was known for. (He knew this because he had once bred them for the army, and that was what the officers wanted: a comfortable time in the saddle.) Besides, he had spotted something in the smaller horse. Not so stylish in appearance as the other, but Grimm's experienced eye had detected that the animal had a streak of quarter in him. The quarter-horse was the fastest breed in the States over its distance, and Grimm knew it.

He untied the reins and patted the smaller animal, getting close as he did so, in order that the creature could smell his new rider, hear his voice and learn he was no threat.

Then he was in the saddle and away.

There was one thought on his mind. The schmuck creating dust ahead of him had had a rifle, and could have been the one who had killed his Andalusian. There again, maybe it was one of the others. Maybe — but that didn't matter now. Grimm couldn't wreak his vengeance on them; they had already paid the price.

At first the rider was a speck in the distance, but as the image got larger, Grimm knew he had chosen the right horse. Whatever the exact percentage of quarter-horse coursing through the animal's veins, it was enough to give him the edge.

Some ten minutes on, Grimm noted that the trail ahead dropped sharply and he watched the rider disappear from view over the edge. It was a minute or so before he got to the same point. He smiled when he reined in and looked down. The grade was quite steep and needed caution. But the same panic that had led the man to give up his advantage with the long gun in town was still manifest: instead of negotiating the incline with care, he had sent his steed hurtling down.

Now he was on his knees in the scree less than half-way down, his horse cantering riderless across the distant plain. The horse had lost its footing, and the rider had been thrown. The man staggered to his feet, saw his pursuer, and began lurching clumsily down the grade. Grimm allowed the palomino to make its descent at its own pace. On the flat, he gigged his mount to pick up speed.

The man threw glances back as he ran, finally stopping when he realized the futility of attempting to escape with no horse and no cover. He waited while the hunter neared.

Grimm reined in some twenty yards away. He dismounted and resumed the unrelenting advance that had marked his walk along Main Street.

'What you gonna do?' the man yelled.

Grimm ignored the question, without faltering in his purposeful gait. 'Who's behind this? Who's paying you cruds?'

'It's more than my life's worth to tell you, mister.'

'You're in a bind, pal. It's your life's

worth *not* to tell me.'

The man watched him with expanding eyes, then hauled on his pistol butt. But both Grimm's guns were already out and spitting fire. The man spread-eagled in mid-air and careered backwards. Grimm kept on walking and firing — until he was standing with empty guns over the body.

'You wanna know what am I gonna do? *That*'s what I'm gonna do,' he told the bloodied corpse.

He had killed many men throughout the years, but only under two circumstances: as a soldier in the line of duty, and as a bounty-hunter in self-defence. This was the first time he had killed beyond those bounds. However, it was not in cold blood. Grimm had blasted the life out of this son of a bitch in *hot* blood.

Yet the impassive aspect of his features as he looked down at the dead man betrayed no evidence that such thoughts had even entered his head. The son of a bitch needed killing for what he had done — and that was that.

He strolled back to the palomino and hauled himself into the saddle.

⋆　⋆　⋆

Back in town, there was a large crowd round the scene. The two bodies had been placed neatly, side by side, near the boardwalk. The lawman was standing beside Kelly, whom he had roped to a stanchion.

'You get him?' the sheriff asked.

'I got him,' Grimm said, as he drew rein. 'He ain't gonna shoot no more horses.'

He dismounted. 'Must say, Sheriff — if this is your regular welcoming committee for strangers, it suffers from certain deficiencies.'

'Who were those men?' the lawman asked.

Then, for the first time, Grimm realized he had missed the opportunity of getting the information out of the fellow out on the plain. The man had started bantering when the question had been asked, and the emotion that had fuelled Grimm's actions had allowed for no chit-chat. He gave the corpses the once-over. Didn't recognize them. He threw a glance at his captive.

'You saw it all. Any ideas?' he asked.

Kelly shook his head.

'You sure you don't recognize 'em?'

The man shook his head again.

'Despite what you say, I figure it was some of your pals,' Grimm opined. 'It was plain they were after me, not you.'

He crossed to his Andalusian, and began unstrapping the saddle and caparisons.

When he had finished, he looked up at the silent crowd. 'Nobody's gonna make steaks and glue outa him. I want him buried with some dignity. Who's got a shovel and can handle it?'

A couple of labourers stepped forward.

'A horse is quite a weight,' Grimm sighed. 'The job's gonna take more than two.' Another couple offered their services, and he pushed some bills into their hands.

'OK, move quick. I don't want rigor setting in and some chowderhead having to break his legs to get him in the hole. And move your asses, because I ain't gonna be in town for long. Let me know when you've finished, so I can see the job's done.'

He looked across the drag and noted the name on the false-front, DESTINY HOTEL & SALOON.

'You'll find me in the drinking-parlour yonder.'

'Hold it there, stranger,' the sheriff said, as Grimm untied the rope fixing his captive to the stanchion. 'I got some questions need answering.'

'You got two questions,' Grimm said wearily. 'Who are the stiffs laid out there, and what's it all about? The answer's 'I don't know' in both cases. As for me, the name's Grimm, and I've been commissioned by the town council of Lobo Wells to take this fellow in. I come into your burgh, and I get jumped and get

163

my hoss shot from under me. That's all I know. Now, I need some relaxation and refreshment.' He nodded to the corpses. 'Meantimes, you got some garbage that needs removing from your street, Sheriff.'

After he had retrieved his jacket and hat from the clothes-store, the operation of donning the jacket reminded him of the stinging in his shoulder. He could live with it, but it was greatly blooded, and he'd been around long enough to know that even slight wounds need tending. As he mounted the boardwalk, he noted a young boy standing close, his eyes still wide at the scene he had seen played out before him.

'You know the doctor's place, son?' Grimm asked.

'Yes, sir.'

Grimm slipped a coin into the lad's hand. 'Tell him he's got a patient in the drinking parlour. There's another dime waiting for you when he turns up.'

With that, he escorted his prisoner

into the saloon and ordered two sarsaparillas, taking up residence at a table that enabled him to have his back to the wall while he faced the batwings.

He eased off his jacket in readiness, then took out his pipe and teased tobacco out of his pouch. He'd just got a good blaze going in his pipe, when the doctor made an appearance.

'Despite what you say,' Kelly said to Grimm, as the medic made his examination, 'I didn't know the varmints. On the other hand, the way I was trussed up I was a sitting duck. They could have put my lights out anytime, but they didn't bother. So, like you said, it was you they were after. Why?'

'Huh,' the Reaper grunted, philosophically regarding the smoke rising from his briar. 'I been throwing a rope round renegades since the War Between the States. That's a hell of a time. There's a whole passel of bozos out there with my name on one of their bullets. Who knows? Comes with the territory. Maybe that's what this was about.'

The doctor squinted his eyes and wrinkled his nose in distaste as he went about his business, wreathed in smoke from the hunter's pipe. But there was something about this particular patient that militated against the practitioner voicing any complaints about the noxious fumes.

He called for a basin of warm water. Some fifteen minutes later, the basin's contents were deep red and the bandages in place.

'Minor wound,' he said, surveying the result. 'Obviously it'll be painful for a spell but it should be no problem if you keep it clean.' He nodded at the bowl. 'Needless to say, you've lost some blood and need to rest up.'

'Ain't got time, Doc,' Grimm replied, standing in order that he could don his jacket once more. But his head spun, and he fell back into the chair.

'As you can see,' the doctor observed, 'it's a matter of necessity, not choice. The body needs to rest to make up the deficiency. A day or so.'

Grimm exhaled noisily at the prospect. 'Will an overnight rest-up do?'

The doctor pulled a wry face. 'Could do.'

Grimm grunted in frustration and looked over at the man behind the bar. 'You got a place at this Destiny Hotel of yours?'

The proprietor raised his hands in a welcoming gesture.

'Every room's vacant at the moment, sir. So you've got the pick of our accommodation.'

Grimm paid the doctor's bill, and the man was closing his bag when the sheriff came in.

'Mr Grimm. Seems there was a fourth guy.'

'How d'you know?' Grimm asked, through teeth clenched on his pipe-stem.

'Immediately after the shooting, someone saw a fellow come from round the back at the other end of town. Sent a signal via the telegraph, then lit out.'

The Reaper nodded in realization.

'Mmm, I saw him, too. Longways down the drag. But the direction he was headed in, I didn't peg him to be with the same outfit.'

'Yeah,' the sheriff said, handing him a pencilled note. 'This is what the operator sent.'

The telegraph was addressed to Jed Martin, and read: 'Coming back. Ned and Woody out of the frame.'

Grimm returned the paper. 'At least you got names for your corpses. Ned and Woody, whoever they are. And I got the name of somebody who wants me planted.'

'This Jed Martin?' the sheriff posed.

'Yeah, seems like it.'

'And who's he?'

'Father of the guy killed by Kelly here, my prisoner.'

The sheriff looked puzzled. 'Well, if revenge is his motive, how come he sent guys to kill you' — he then nodded towards Kelly — 'and not him?'

'You got me beat, Sheriff.'

12

At the far end of Lobo Wells, behind a building, and so unseen from the town, stood four men. At their centre was Jed Martin. The worm of vengeance gnawed at him, and he was being thwarted by this bounty-hunter from nowhere. He needed to know more about him, to find a weak link.

'Leave it to me, boss.' It was Gaff. He was a huge man, with the roughed-up features of a man who is no stranger to a fist-fight, or of someone who has run head-on into a few barn doors. 'I'll get the information out of some dirt-grubber,' he went on confidently.

'Like hell you will,' Martin grunted. 'This calls for something subtle, you big lunk.' He turned to one of the other men, a young, long-necked fellow with all the appearance of a no-account cow-puncher. But his looks belied his history. He was a bundle of trouble, wanted in the neighbouring state for a string of offences. Being part of the Martin outfit served doubly to provide him with employment, while also keeping him away from the eagle eyes of the authorities across the state line.

'Fan-Tan,' Martin said, 'they don't know you in town. I want you to mosey in and see what you can find out about this Grimm. What's his background, why he was in town, and such. And take it easy, act casual.'

★   ★   ★

The air of The Golden Dollar was heavy with cigarette smoke and a general odour of liquor. The batwings creaked open and a young fellow entered. Tel, the bartender, looked up from the glass he was polishing, and didn't recognize the man. He placed the glass on a shelf.

'What'll it be, sir?'

'I'll skip the drinks, friend,' Fan-Tan

said. 'It's just information I want.'

'I'll oblige if I can, sir.'

'What do you know about this Jonathan Grimm?'

The bartender pulled a wry face. Immediately he hazarded a guess that there was a connection between this young fellow and Jed Martin, on the strength that Martin would be the only man in town with a interest in the bounty-hunter. To the outside world, Martin was a man of probity and virtue. However, there are certain posts in any town that provide their holders with an automatic finger on the pulse of what's going on, and bartending is one of them. In this way, Tel had heard there was more to the respectable Mr Martin than met the eye, something shady. That beneath the exterior, the man was hard and could mean trouble. On the other hand, he knew little of this Grimm, other than that he was an affable oldster. But more importantly, he knew he was a friend to some regular customers. And that was enough reason to be wary, so he replied, 'Can't say I recognize the name, sir.'

Fan-Tan remembered what his boss had told him about playing it cool, and hid his irritation. He turned from the bar and looked at the remaining patrons, one at the counter, some at tables, a couple in a booth.

'Say, any of you guys know of this Grimm? Stranger in town. Heard tell he used this place a couple of times.'

Again, no response.

'Old feller, tall,' he continued, touching his cheekbone. 'They tell me he's got a scatter of powder-burns here.'

One of the customers in the booth raised a hand. 'Why, yes, pal. There has been such a feller in here.'

'What do you know of him?'

The man shrugged. 'Nothing, save he came in with a group of carousers. Seems he was in town to attend a wedding.'

'What else can you tell me about him?'

'That's it, sir. We didn't have much truck with him, did we, fellers?'

'Attending a wedding, eh?' Fan-Tan said. He contemplated for a moment, then touched his hat. 'Much obliged, boys.'

Outside, he stood on the boardwalk for a time, then headed towards the church, past stores, then clapboard houses. His boss needed to get something on the man, and this wedding thing might provide a link.

At the church, he put on his politest demeanour and asked the reverend the same question.

'Grimm?' the man said. 'The name rings a bell. However, it has been my privilege to bless many weddings recently, so I cannot be specific.'

'You keep records?'

'Yes, there might be something there. If you will come with me.'

In the vestry, he drew a book from a drawer and placed it on the table. He opened it and ran his finger along the lines of recent entries.

'There!' he said triumphantly. 'Jonathan Grimm. Witness to a wedding. Ah, yes, I remember now. The Stanhope girl.'

Fan-Tan studied the indicated signature. 'What was his connection?'

'Mr Grimm gave away the bride.'

'So that means he's kin?'

'Not necessarily. Might be distant family. All I know is, he acted in that capacity in lieu of her father, Jim Stanhope. Poor fellow passed on some time back. You might have known him.'

Fan-Tan shook his head. His mind worked on what he had learned. Whether or not Grimm was family, to have come some distance to give away the bride meant there had to be some strong emotional link.

'The happy couple,' he said, 'did they move away or stay hereabouts?'

'Afraid I wasn't privy to their plans.'

'Well, thank you, Reverend. You've been very helpful.'

Outside, he replaced his hat. There'll be one place in town where they know *everybody*'s business, he thought to himself; the old biddies round the cracker-barrel in the grocery store.

He was right. There were several women in there gossiping, and he soon found out that the newly-weds were living in a place close to the Stanhope homestead. And the town hens were happy to give him very precise directions as to its location. Which he was equally happy to relate eventually to his waiting boss.

★　★　★

The amber of twilight lay on the land as the four riders approached. They reined in a hundred yards from the shack and tied their horses to a clump of sage.

'Tend to the broncs, Clancy,' Martin whispered to one of them.

Clancy, a man of indeterminate age, with mutton-chop whiskers and a face made lopsided by a saddle-bag under one eye, did as he was bid, then watched the other three advance a little and take cover.

According to their information, there were only the young woman and her husband dwelling there. They watched for a while, then worked their way close to the house. At a window, they could hear a male and a female voice.

'There's just the two of them in there, boss,' Gaff whispered. 'Let's just go in and grab her.'

'Whoa there, big boy,' Martin countered. 'I often find on some matters it pays to wait a while; to see if an opportunity presents itself.'

He was right. Barely a few minutes later, the back door opened and Frank came out with a bowl of dirty water. He walked into the darkness and emptied the container. He turned and had gone but a few paces, when something whacked him hard on the back of the head.

Gaff didn't need to check the man was out — it was his experience that few remained conscious after one of his blows, especially when delivered with a huge hunk of wood — but Martin insisted he confirm the fact. When he had done so, the group headed for the lighted doorway. The rest was equally easy.

★   ★   ★

Next morning, the bounty-hunter was reasonably recovered and taking a final rest in the lobby of the Destiny Hotel in preparation for departure, when a figure made an appearance at the entrance.

'Anybody here by the name of Grimm?'

The Reaper looked up. There was a fellow standing in the half-open batwings. Looked like a telegraph-operator. Grimm was beginning to recognize the breed. He raised his hand. 'Here, pal.'

The man came across and handed him a piece of paper.

Out came the glasses. 'Sorry you didn't settle for deal,' the message said. 'New arrangement. Now have my own package.' Grimm's blood froze when he read the ensuing words. 'Name of Sarah. Trade one for one. Don't bring anybody else along. You know what I mean. Else you never see your merchandise again. Jed Martin.'

'Any reply, sir?'

Grimm didn't properly hear the man as he reread the ominous words. Then he became aware of his presence, and said, 'Reply? Yes, but later. This needs thinking on.'

'Very well, sir. When you're ready, the office is left, and a couple of blocks down the drag.'

'What's it say?' Kelly asked.

Grimm spoke very slowly. 'Somebody wants you real bad.' He packed his glasses away and looked at his captive. 'This Jed Martin. He's some hell of a bastard.'

'You're telling me.'

'What angle is he playing? What do you know about him?'

'Like you say, a genuine son of a bitch. Father and son alike.'

'Time for some straight talking. This

story you been trying to tell me, let me have it now.'

'I ain't saying I been a choirboy, Mr Grimm. I admit it, I crossed to the wrong side of the tracks in my early days, but I been trying to go straight in recent times. Like I been telling you.'

'Yeah,' Grimm said impatiently. 'I know, you been blabbing ever since I clapped the irons on you, but I ain't been listening. Now I am. Go on.'

'I been a hellion. Ain't gainsaying that. Got a temper, always getting into scrapes. As a youngster I've thieved, put my hand to rustling. And I've served time. My second stretch was two years, for trying to knock-over a stagecoach.'

'That's the larceny poster.'

'Yeah. But during that last time in Territorial Pen, something happened. I figure I grew up. You know the way things can happen. So, I kept my nose clean, learned to hold my temper, and they let me out with six months off for good behaviour. Well, I reckoned I couldn't go on like I had been. Finally saw that if I was to make anything of my life, I'd have to go straight. Ended up in Gulch City. Got myself in with an outfit cattle-droving out there. Then I met Lizzie.'

'Lizzie?'

'My girl. We set up home together. She paid no never-mind to my past. Said it was what I was *now* that counted. She's a real gem, Mr Grimm. Got faith in me. I think that's what I needed. A gal to believe in me. Money was no great shakes, but by then I'd realized that that's the price you pay for going straight. It was hunky-dory for a spell until I got laid off after a drive. But she was great over that, too. She said it was only a matter of time before I got fixed up with another job and we could lead a regular life. Get married and have kids.'

The tone of his voice changed. 'Then I ran into Sonny Martin in Lobo Wells. When he learned I was out of work, he offered me a place over at his pa's spread. The Big M. It wasn't until I'd got settled into the bunk-house there that I found out what the job was. Jed Martin, big cheese in the territory. Straight-up, respectable citizen — *huh*! You know what he does? Uses the ranch as a front for long-riding. His boys ride out of state and knock-over banks, trains, and such like. The jobs are planned down to the last detail. After a knock-over, the boys high-tail it back to the ranch and play at being cowboys, till the heat's off and the next job has been set up. It became plain that Sonny only took me on the payroll because he thought I was a no-good like him and the others.

'When I learned the set-up, I told him I'd turned over a new leaf, and then went back to my girl's. Afore I knowed what had happened he'd come over to Gulch with some of his heavies, and beat me up. Whacked me so hard I flaked out.'

His voice faltered. 'When I came to, he'd raped my girl. Told her she'd get more of the same if I opened my mouth about the Martin set-up. Like I said, I got a temper, and I just blew. I lit out to Lobo Wells. Make no mistake, Mr Grimm, I meant to kill him but in a fair face-up. And that's what happened.

'They're trying to nail me for plugging the sheriff, too. But I didn't shoot him. That was one of Sonny's shots going wild. I couldn't have plugged the sheriff. He was *behind* me. I planted Sonny all right. Ain't denying that. But it was a straight man-to-man shoot-out. But it ain't right they should try and peg me for putting a slug in the sheriff. There were enough folks watching. Must be somebody prepared to vouch it was one of Sonny's slugs winged the sheriff, and not one of mine.'

'I know,' Grimm said. 'I was there, saw it.' Then, after some reflection: 'But how do I know you're telling the truth about the other stuff?'

Kelly shrugged. 'You don't.'

Grimm pondered on the man's words. 'How many jobs the Martin gang pull?'

'Dunno. I wasn't there long enough to know about their activities in detail.'

'So you can't tie them down to a particular heist?'

'Sonny told me of a couple. Was bragging about how much money they pulled, when he was dangling the honeypot in front of me. He was being open, thinking I was the same breed as them, me having done stir and all.'

Awkwardly he took the makings from his pocket.

'Here,' Grimm said, taking the package and proceeding to build the man a smoke.

Kelly watched him. 'You know the Continental railroad a hundred miles north of here?'

'I know of it, but not in detail. I ain't local.'

'Big robbery there a month back. Cattlemen's payroll. He was bragging that was them. And the Madre Bank job over the state line afore that.'

'I heard of that one. Big dollars. Man killed.'

'Huh, there was *two* killed on the Continental job. One of the conductors, and one of the rail-road's armed guards.'

Grimm nodded. 'This means there'll be dodgers posted.'

The other took the proffered cigarette. 'Yeah,' he said, when he had taken a drag, 'but dodgers ain't much good if there's no names on 'em. The way they plan their capers and operate long-riding out of state, nobody knows it's them.'

'*We* know,' Grimm grunted. He pondered on the information. 'If there weren't complications, somebody could pull a packet on these yahoos,' he went on, in a low tone more to himself. 'But I gotta forget all that. Sarah comes first. Ain't thinking of nothing but Sarah.'

He thought some more. 'The main thing is, from what you've told me, I have a picture of the kind of hardcases I'm up against. If I didn't know already.'

'Who's this Sarah you mentioned?' Kelly asked.

Grimm handed him the telegraph message. 'Someone close. Martin must have found out my connection with her. Reckon you might call her my step-daughter. Fact is, her getting married was my reason for coming to Lobo Wells in the first place.'

'So, Martin's got her,' Kelly said after he'd read it. 'What you gonna do?'

'The way I see it, I take you to him, hand you over, and hope he doesn't pull any stunts. If it's a genuine offer, I do the swap and Sarah should be safe.'

'But he's gonna kill me, Mr Grimm. You've seen what he's capable of.'

'I gotta think of Sarah first and foremost.'

'I tell you, he's gonna kill me. He doesn't want you taking me to the law because he knows the stuff about his racket will come out in court. On top of that, he not only wants me dead for planting Sonny — but he's all fired up to do it himself!'

'That *shouldn't* be my problem.'

'Shouldn't?' Kelly repeated.

'Yeah,' Grimm sighed. 'The hell of it is, I'm beginning to believe your story. Jed Martin's shown what kind of man he is by sending heavies out to kill me. That's some evidence in support of what you're telling me.'

'So we're back to what you gonna do. My life's in your hands, Mr Grimm.'

'I don't have to be a college professor to know *my* life's at stake, too, not that it matters. From what I know of this Martin, he'll probably want to finish me for planting three of his cronies.'

He began stoking up his pipe. 'Well, from my understanding of the whole shebang, looks like you were justified in wiping Sonny Martin off the map.' He slowly tamped down the tobacco while he thought. 'All I care about now is Sarah. If I cut you some slack, and you *help* me in seeing Sarah safe, I'll have no reason to take you in. After that, you take your chances.'

'I'll do anything you say, Mr Grimm.'

Grimm motioned him to put forward his hands, and he unlocked the shackles. 'You know I won't chase you now I've got Sarah on my mind, so there's nothing stopping you from scatting right now. But I'm putting some faith in you.'

'Don't worry on that score,' Kelly said, rubbing his wrists. 'I'm with you, Mr Grimm.'

'Right, kid, your showdown with Sonny Martin tells me you're OK with a gun.'

Kelly continued rubbing his wrists. 'Well, that was the first face-to-face situation I've been in. I'm no gun-slick, but I can handle one.'

'Good. Those two stiffs from yesterday, over in the funeral parlour, they had armoury. Take your pick from what they were carrying.' He thought some more. 'Now, you've been to Martin's place, tell me about it.'

'A big spread, about five miles west of Lobo Wells.'

'How many men has he got?'

'There's quite a number. Maybe fifteen or so. But they're concerned with the legitimate beef business. It's only the small group around the old man that knows about the heists.'

'This inner circle — how many?'

Kelly counted on his fingers. 'Could be around eight. But Sonny's gone. Three down today.'

'Well, if we start with your estimate of eight, there's four left. The one who got away — it's gonna take him a day to get back. That means at the moment Martin's got a back-up of three.' He examined the tobacco in his pipe before lighting it. 'How come you didn't recognize the two in town today?'

'I wasn't at Martin's place long, and there were two of the gang I didn't see. They were out on a job someplace. Now the pieces are fitting together, on reflection, the names on the cable do seem a mite familiar. I figure they must be the two of the gang I didn't clap eyes on.'

Grimm pondered. 'So, including the boss, we'll be facing a total of four. Now, the showdown mustn't take place

on his home ground. But where else?'
He lit the tobacco, and puffed the thing
into a vigorous conflagration, eventually
coming out with, 'Figure I know *just*
the place.'

★   ★   ★

Over in the telegraph office, Grimm
sent a message: 'Will do swap at cabin.
Red Mountain Mine. Two days from
now.'

His suffering of Ol' Barnaby's dron-
ings hadn't been a complete waste of
time, after all.

13

Jed Martin reined in and angled his head to read the sign half-hanging between a couple of posts.

'Red Mountain Mine,' he read aloud. 'Figure this is the place the bounty-chaser meant.'

He looked along the rutted track that cut away from the main trail. It sloped gently down to an arroyo, across which there must have been a bridge at one time, then up towards the mountain. Even from this distance, the darkness of an opening in the steep slope was visible, and, around it, the rusting detritus of excavation.

He took in the shack and surrounding valley. Then he looked back up the trail along which they had just come.

Finally, he turned to his men. 'Grimm will be coming the same way. So, Clancy, you ride back up the trail to the ridge. Hide yourself away and keep watch. Wave when you see him coming. Meanwhile, you two, come with me.'

He rode to the shack and dismounted. They tied up their horses, and Martin entered the cabin. After he had made an inspection of the interior, he emerged and looked at Sarah. Her hands were bound in front of her, and the once-neat bun of her red hair was straggly and dust-covered. He nodded to her. 'Make yourself at home, gal.'

Fan-Tan helped her down, and she went in, to drop exhausted on a cot.

Martin walked clear of the awning and stood in the foreyard, surveying the environs.

'Think this Grimm'll bring the law, boss?' Gaff asked.

'No way. He values that she-kitty too much, and he knows what would happen to her if he did.'

He started building himself a smoke, and Gaff asked, 'We just gonna make a straight swap?'

'Don't be stupid,' Martin growled.

'Kelly has spent quite a spell with this bounty-chaser. That's plenty of time for him to have told him all about us and our operations. You can bet your bottom dollar on that. So, once we've got our hands on Kelly, this Grimm will have to be removed.' He looked around at the bleakness of the terrain. 'Out in the wilderness here, nobody will ever know.'

'Out here, yes. But they can still tie this business in to us back at Lobo Wells.'

'Like hell they can,' Martin snarled. 'Nobody in town knows Fan-Tan. A stranger asks questions, so what? And that guy at the gal's house doesn't know what hit him, never mind *who* hit him. So there's nothing to tie us in.'

'What about the telegraph-operator?'

Martin waved his completed cigarette to make his point. 'Didn't we take the copies of our messages? All there is, is his word. But he's got a wife and kids, and I made it clear what would happen to them if he blabs. So we got a clean slate on the matter. To boot, back at Lobo Wells, the sheriff's on his sickbed. So there's no law to do any investigating or punishing, anyways.'

'And the girl?' Fan-Tan pressed, in a speculative, musing voice.

Martin lit his cigarette without answering. He'd heard the question, but ignored it, the answer being obvious to both men. Instead, he turned his mind to Grimm and said, 'Figure the bozo won't be here for a couple of hours, so you pair have got time to have a bite to eat and wet your whistles. When you've done that, take cover on separate sides of the shack. It's my reckoning he will be going for a straight swap on account of the girl. But keep your eyes open, 'cos we gotta be prepared for any tricks.'

Inside, Sarah's eyes were drooping. They'd bivouacked on the way out, but she hadn't been able to sleep, and the deprivation was now catching up with her. As had happened many times over the intervening years, her mind went back to when she was a child and the last time she had seen Mr Grimm. When he had left her with her new foster parents, all those years ago . . .

He explained to her that he had to leave and go about his business. But he would not forget her, and would send her a letter from time to time. After he'd saddled his horse, she had watched him take her new foster father to one side. The tall, mysterious rider pulled out a wad of bills.

'There's nearly a thousand bucks there,' he said, handing it to the homesteader.

'I can't take that, Jonathan.'

'You can, and you will, 'Grimm insisted. 'With me, big money comes and goes. I'm putting it in your hands, as Sarah's guardians. It's yours to do with as you will. What you don't spend in raising the girl, put on one side for when she's older.'

After he'd made his formal goodbyes to the couple, they stood on the veranda with Sarah between them. As

Grimm made a final check on the cinch, the girl broke free from the caring hands, run forward and came to a stand-still in the open space, half-way between the readied horses and the building, clutching her blue-dressed doll.

Grimm saw her movement, and walked back to her. Gawkily, he put his arms around her and pulled her to him for a moment. She was not to know that he hadn't held someone close like that for a long time, and that there was an unfamiliar, and uncomfortable, lump in his throat.

He whispered something, but she couldn't remember what it was.

Then he held her at arm's length, and looked into her eyes. But he could tell she didn't have much understanding of what he had said or of what was going on. She was only a kid.

She didn't speak, just backed away a few paces, still clutching the doll. He hauled himself into the saddle, and nudged the Andalusian. He turned *once, gave a last wave and headed out. Yeah, she was only a kid, and she wouldn't understand the way he felt.*

However, that she did bear him similar feelings was indicated by the faint, sad smile that came to her lips as she returned his wave.

But, by then, he was too far away to see . . .

Her reverie was broken by Martin clumping in and dropping heavily into a rickety chair.

'You sure my Frank's all right?' she asked.

'For the tenth time, woman,' Martin snapped, 'he'll wake up with a headache, is all. Now quit squawking.'

At first, she hadn't known what was going on — being gagged and dragged out of her house in the middle of the night — but during the ride out she had picked up enough from the interchange between the four men to learn that she was being used in some sort of exchange. And she'd also heard enough for her to know not to trust any one of them.

14

They had started out at dawn, Grimm riding the palomino. Two days on, he reined in when he recognized the trail close to Red Mountain.

'The cabin is over the next ridge at the foot of the mountain,' he said. 'They'll have got there ahead of us and be settled in.'

'Are you going to be OK, Mr Grimm?' Kelly interrupted, looking into the weary eyes. For some time he'd noticed the old man swaying slightly in the saddle.

Grimm made a dismissive gesture with his hand, and continued: 'Now, they'll be expecting us from the east, and they'll certainly have a lookout. So we'll circle round and come in from the west.'

He wheeled his horse off the trail and cut across the rough grass. Half an hour later they were approaching from the opposite direction. They dismounted and tethered the horses to a cotton-wood out of sight. Moving cautiously on foot, they stopped when they got a good view of the cabin and area.

They could see two men in front of the building. Grimm squinted at the horses under the awning, but their images were difficult to distinguish from their surroundings.

'Your eyes are younger than mine. How many horses can you make out?'

'Five,' replied Kelly.

'One each for Martin and Sarah. 'That leaves another three. So, there's four varmints in total. Seems your estimate was right.' He mused on the figure. 'Two against four. I've faced worse odds.'

'Speak for yourself.'

'Listen, everything's gonna be OK, kid. We've avoided their lookout, so we've got the element of surprise.' He looked down at the cabin again. 'Now, we can see two guys. Martin will be in the cabin with Sarah, and there'll be the lookout man up the trail.'

'So, what do we do?'

'I know this place. See the arroyo that runs the length of the valley? Midway, there's a secret tunnel connecting it to the shack. I'm gonna make my entry from there. But I need a diversion. This calls for the oldest trick in the book.'

He licked his finger and put it to the wind. 'If we light fires this end of the valley, they won't smell the smoke. Then we drop some cartridges into them.'

He pulled his Bowie knife and began hacking at semi-dead vegetation. Kelly joined him, using his bare hands. When they had a significant mound, Grimm moved off. A hundred yards on, he repeated the process.

He took a box of shells from his saddle-bag. He extracted a handful and pushed them into the man's pocket. 'Those are for the Winchester. You got enough left in the box for a hell of a racket. Start the fires now.'

He moved back to their vantage position and pointed. 'I'm going to make my way along the arroyo. You'll be able to see me from here. Give me time to get into the tunnel and to make some progress along it. Then, drop the rounds into the fire and start moving around the perimeter of the valley.'

Grimm pulled his Winchester from its scabbard and handed it to the other. 'When you hear the shells exploding, start loosing off your own gun, randomly from under cover. That way they'll be hearing shots from at least three directions, and it should maximize their confusion. Keep your eye on the far trail. When the fourth man shows himself, start moving down.'

Kelly stuck out his hand. 'Good luck.'

Grimm shook it, then moved to the ridge and began to work his way down, moving from one cover to another. When he made it to the arroyo, he rolled into it, but the drop was more than he had anticipated, and he lay for a few seconds silently groaning at the strain on his joints. Getting to his feet, he felt dizzy again. He leant against the arroyo wall and pushed his hand under the shoulder of his jacket. The crimson hand he withdrew told him that was it: his wound had reopened. He remained for a time composing himself, then staggered towards the shack, keeping to the side.

Kelly had waited until he saw Grimm drop out of sight into the arroyo, then got himself a fistful of shells. He jiggled the cartridges restlessly in his hand as he imagined the man now moving along the dry bed of the watercourse.

Eventually, Grimm found the bush that Ol' Barnaby had shown him. Pulling it aside, he bent down and entered the tunnel. His ancient knees creaked as he worked his way along. The original construction hadn't catered for a man of his size. The air was musty, stifling. Twenty feet in, his passage was blocked. Although he was in pitch darkness, he knew there must have been some kind of collapse.

Returning was not an option, so he began to scoop away the material. After minutes of feverish labour, he groped ahead with an extended arm and sensed he had made a breakthrough. He lit a match — yes, he was through. He scraped back more soil and clay to make room, but it was still a tight squeeze. He persevered, and slowly wormed his way through the gap.

Meanwhile, Kelly figured he had given Grimm enough time to get to the tunnel that he had described, so he dropped the shells into the fire. He picked up the rifle and, keeping to cover, loped along the craggy jumble of the valley side to the second fire. After repeating the exercise with another load of shells, he continued his progress, just down from the top.

In the tunnel, Grimm found that once past the first blockage, the passage was relatively clear from then on. He shuffled along until he sensed sounds, indistinct, but unmistakably voices. He pressed on through the darkness only to hit another blockage. But this time, he could hear the voices quite plainly.

Kelly was three parts along the valley when the first of the shells in the fires crackled. He came to standstill and flattened himself against a tree to monitor the effects.

The two men in the foreyard split, one going for the cover of the cabin wall, while the other dashed for the door. Both of them started to throw lead in the direction of the crackling gunfire.

Kelly watched the cabin for a spell, hoping Grimm was in a position to take advantage of the diversion. Then he moved round the tree and began to work his way down.

To his left, a man broke out of the trees at the top of the steep slope. That would be the lookout.

Kelly watched him. He raised his rifle and followed the man, the length of his barrel moving determinedly. Judging he was in range, Kelly pulled the trigger. Dust gouted up behind the figure.

Hell, he should have impressed more on Grimm that he had never been a rifleman! The man broke into a run and made it to the foreyard, diving behind a squat wagon chassis without wheels.

Kelly heard shouts as he jacked in another load. Keeping to cover, he scrambled his way further down. The next time he looked, he was glad to see that the fellow was loosing off shots towards the other end of the valley. That meant he hadn't been located. He descended further, but had to break cover.

As he neared the foreyard, someone shouted, 'There's the bastard!'

He dived to the ground, rifle-fire crackling in his direction. He pulled the trigger again. The mutton-whiskered man behind the wagon yelled and hit the ground, then writhed and became still. Kelly smiled when he recognized the inert face as that of Clancy.

Underground, still faced with the new blockage, Grimm heard shots. That had to mean that he was at the end of the tunnel. Arthritic fingers scraped at the roof as he sought the trapdoor.

Meanwhile, out of rifle shells, Kelly cast aside the Winchester and limber-legged towards the shack. However, its nearside was masked by a stand of small aspens, and he didn't see Gaff behind them. The big man took a bead and fired. It took Kelly in the leg, bringing him down.

Now Kelly was not a practised gunman, but his short life of crime had taught him two things: not to be fazed by action, and to keep going under duress. With this schooling, he used the impetus of his collapse to roll while simultaneously looking for his attacker. Furthermore, although he was no gun-slick, the four-square ox of the man being revealed to him from behind the trees as he rolled, was too big to miss. He pulled his gun and fired from his grounded position.

Despite his weight, the man spun like a top, then spilled clear of the building, arms out-flung. Again Kelly felt satisfaction when he realized it was the brutish Gaff he had put paid to.

Below ground, Grimm fought on. Blind, he explored the roof, until he felt something flat and hard. The trapdoor. Yes, he was at the end of his journey. Slowly he pushed upwards, and the wooden square began to rise.

Eventually, his eyes were at floor level. He could make out Sarah, her hands roped behind her, in the grip of Martin, who was standing at the door, gun in hand.

Grimm lowered the trapdoor so that he could pull back the hammer on his gun without the click being heard. But by the time he had completed this task, when next he raised the cover, Martin had disappeared outside with his captive. Hell!

Then he heard Martin shout, 'Grimm, I told you not to bring the law!'

The hunter eased himself through the trap and, with clay falling from his clothes, he crossed to the door. He proned himself against the jamb. Martin was some twenty feet away, still holding Sarah fast. But now his gun was levelled at her head!

The boss's eyes shot about the terrain, looking up and down the valley. 'Grimm!' he yelled. 'Wherever you are — time's running out!'

The Reaper weighed up the situation. There was no problem in hitting the bulk of the man. Moreover, at such short range, Grimm knew that even with a handgun, he could hit Martin's gunhand. But the man could easily pull trigger in reflex. That was the dilemma.

Should he call the man's name? There was a chance that, in turning, the man's gun would move from its target. However, there was also the chance the man would be startled, and fire instinctively.

But the Reaper's options fast diminished when the man shouted: 'I'm going to count to three. If you don't show yourself, wherever you are, the girl gets it.'

Nothing for it. Grimm would have to go for the gun. But it had to be the most precise shot he had ever made. Even then, Sarah's life would be in the balance.

Needing to extend his arm, he stepped back, lest he be seen by one of Martin's henchmen.

But his precautionary step was his undoing.

What he didn't know was that the man called Fan-Tan was creeping past a window. And Grimm's slight movement had caught his eye. The gangman fired through the glass, catching Grimm in the hip and he fell against the door. Martin whirled round, saw the Reaper slumped against the woodwork, and fired.

Grimm's gun barked simultaneously and both men hit the ground.

The man at the side window dashed round to check the results. But, coming into the open, Fan-Tan was an easy target for Kelly, who brought him down with one shot, then another, to finish him off.

'Mr Grimm!' Sarah screamed.

She ran back to the building, and dropped beside the fallen bounty-hunter.

Kelly limped over and checked in turn that each of the gang-members, and finally Martin, was dead.

'We got 'em all, Mr Grimm!' he shouted triumphantly.

He crossed over, through the lethal stench of cordite that still hung in the air, and knelt beside Sarah.

'How is he?'

She looked at his smashed hip, and at the blood fast covering his chest. 'He's hurt bad.'

'Is there anything I can do?' Kelly said.

'There is nothing more you can do,' the Reaper whispered. 'You're a good kid, Kelly. You done a good job here today. That'll count for you. I think you're gonna make it. Don't worry, when the facts get out, you'll be cleared . . . '

His voice trailed away, and his eyes flicked towards the girl. 'Sarah . . . ' but his voice faded further, and his eyes closed.

She cradled him in her arms. 'No, no! First Pa, then Papa. Now, please, please — don't *you* leave me!'

Under heavy lids, his eyes fluttered once more towards her.

'Please, please,' she moaned. 'Mr Grimm.' Then, for the first time, she used his given name. 'Jonathan.'

The flicker of a smile crossed his face. 'I never thought I'd hear that word on the lips of a loved one again . . . '

'Don't leave me!'

As he had once held her as a child in his arms, so she held him now.

'Tell Hester,' he murmured, after a while, 'I think it just might have worked.'

'What might have worked?'

The faintest of smiles played momentarily on his lips. 'She'll know.'

There was silence again, then he whispered, 'Listen. Can you hear it?'

'Hear what?'

'Swish . . . swish . . . '

She could hear nothing.

He tried to chuckle, but it came out only as a faint exhalation of breath.

'That dumb nickname they gave me . . . the Reaper . . . Huh, what a moniker . . . never been able to shuck it off . . . '

'Don't talk,' she said. 'Save your strength.'

'But there's a Reaper far more powerful than me,' he whispered. 'The genuine article . . . the Big Casino Reaper . . . and I can hear the swishing of his scythe . . . '

Then his head slumped.

Postscript

As has been noted in earlier books chronicling the life of the man known as 'The Reaper', there is still little known about him — other than a cache of historical documents showing his fading signature on receipts for twenty-three men brought in for bounty payment.

There are some who say that somewhere out in Red Mountain Valley there is a grave. A grave that was originally bedecked by flowers that were picked and arranged by a young, flame-haired newly-wed. But it would be difficult to trace, because it is now overgrown, the wooden marker bearing the name of Jonathan Grimm long since disintegrated.

And yet there are others who say that the old adventurer spent his last days happily, with a certain widow-woman, his now-silent .44s hanging on the homestead wall.

But, whatever the truth, one thing is certain. *This* is where the saga of Jonathan Grimm — Reaper Grimm, the bounty-hunter of legend — finally ends.

We do hope that you have enjoyed reading this large print book.

Did you know that all of our titles are available for purchase?

We publish a wide range of high quality large print books including:
Romances, Mysteries, Classics
General Fiction
Non Fiction and Westerns

Special interest titles available in large print are:
The Little Oxford Dictionary
Music Book, Song Book
Hymn Book, Service Book

Also available from us courtesy of Oxford University Press:
Young Readers' Dictionary
(large print edition)
Young Readers' Thesaurus
(large print edition)

For further information or a free brochure, please contact us at:
Ulverscroft Large Print Books Ltd.,
The Green, Bradgate Road, Anstey,
Leicester, LE7 7FU, England.
Tel: (00 44) **0116 236 4325**
Fax: (00 44) **0116 234 0205**

Other titles in the
Linford Western Library:

SMOKING STAR

B. J. Holmes

In the one-horse town of Medicine Bluff two men were dead. Sheriff Jack Starr didn't need the badge on his chest to spur him into tracking the killer. He had his own reason for seeking justice, a reason no-one knew. It drove him to take a journey into the past where he was to discover something else that was to add even greater urgency to the situation — to stop Montana's rivers running red with blood.

THE WIND WAGON

Troy Howard

Sheriff Al Corning was as tough as they came and with his four seasoned deputies he kept the peace in Laramie — at least until the squatters came. To fend off starvation, the settlers took some cattle off the cowmen, including Jonas Lefler. A hard, unforgiving man, Lefler retaliated with lynchings. Things got worse when one of the squatters revealed he was a former Texas lawman — and no mean shooter. Could Sheriff Corning prevent further bloodshed?